D0880944

JURASSIC PARK

™

VOLUME 2

THE MIRACLE OF CLONING

ADAPTED BY
WALTER SIMONSON,
GIL KANE AND GEORGE PEREZ

Spotlight

IDW

visit us at www.abdopublishing.com

Reinforced library bound editions published in 2014 by Spotlight, a division of the ABDO Group, PO Box 398166, Minneapolis, Minnesota 55439. Published by agreement with IDW Publishing. www.idwpublishing.com

Printed in the United States of America, North Mankato, Minnesota.
052013
092013
♻ This book contains at least 10% recycled materials.

Library of Congress Cataloging-in-Publication Data

Simonson, Walter.
  Jurassic Park / adapted by Walter Simonson, Gil Kane, and George Perez.
    pages cm
  ISBN 978-1-61479-183-6 (vol. 1: Danger) -- ISBN 978-1-61479-184-3 (vol. 2: The miracle of cloning) -- ISBN 978-1-61479-185-0 (vol. 3: Don't move!) -- ISBN 978-1-61479-186-7 (vol. 4: Leaving Jurassic Park)
  1. Graphic novels. I. Kane, Gil. II. Perez, George, 1954- III. Title.
  PZ7.7.S5465Jur 2013
  741.5'973--dc23
                    2013011263

All Spotlight books are reinforced library binding and manufactured in the United States of America.

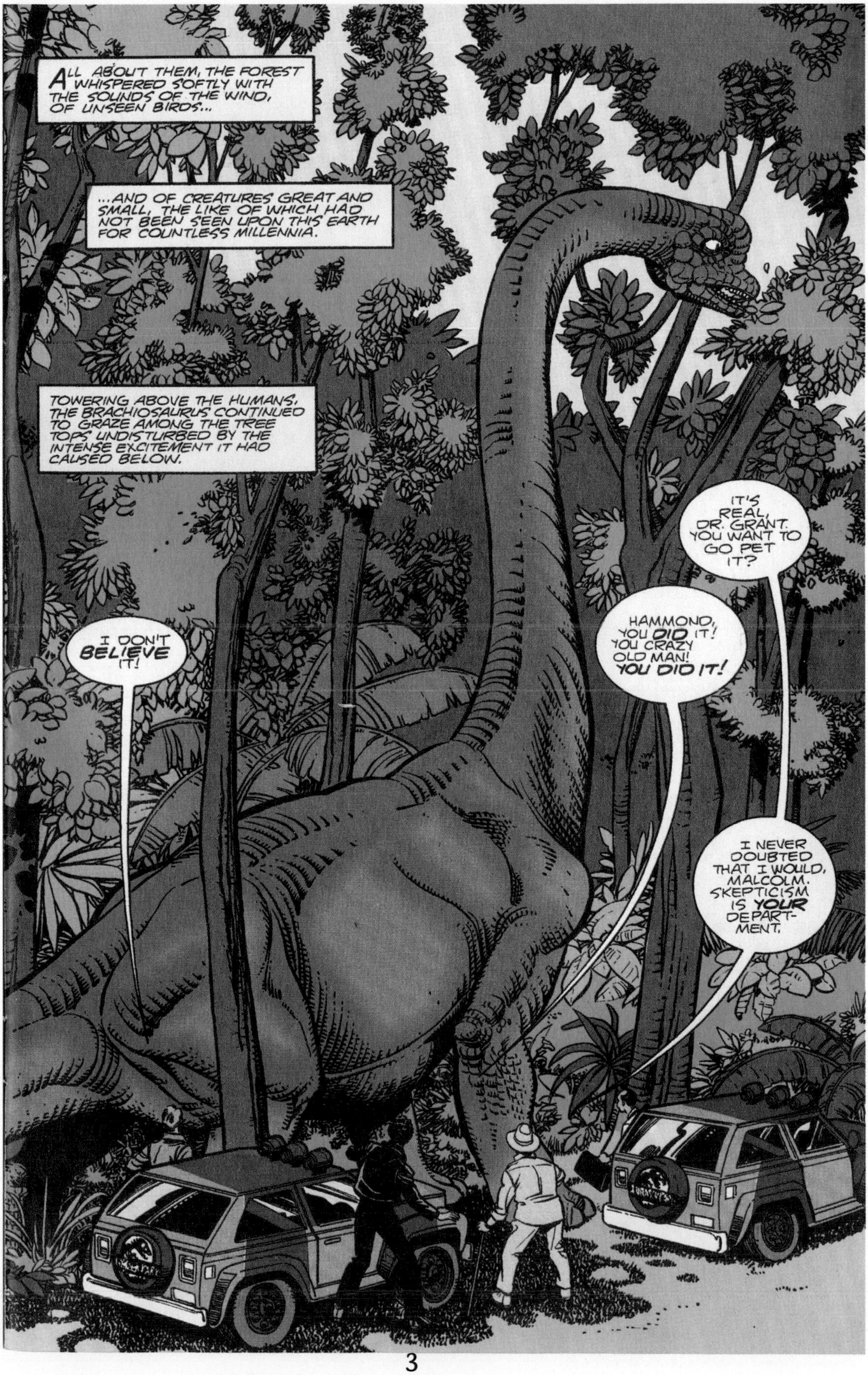
ALL ABOUT THEM, THE FOREST WHISPERED SOFTLY WITH THE SOUNDS OF THE WIND, OF UNSEEN BIRDS...
...AND OF CREATURES GREAT AND SMALL, THE LIKE OF WHICH HAD NOT BEEN SEEN UPON THIS EARTH FOR COUNTLESS MILLENNIA.
TOWERING ABOVE THE HUMANS, THE BRACHIOSAURUS CONTINUED TO GRAZE AMONG THE TREE TOPS UNDISTURBED BY THE INTENSE EXCITEMENT IT HAD CAUSED BELOW.
I DON'T BELIEVE IT!
IT'S REAL, DR. GRANT. YOU WANT TO GO PET IT?
HAMMOND, YOU DID IT! YOU CRAZY OLD MAN! YOU DID IT!
I NEVER DOUBTED THAT I WOULD, MALCOLM. SKEPTICISM IS YOUR DEPART-MENT.

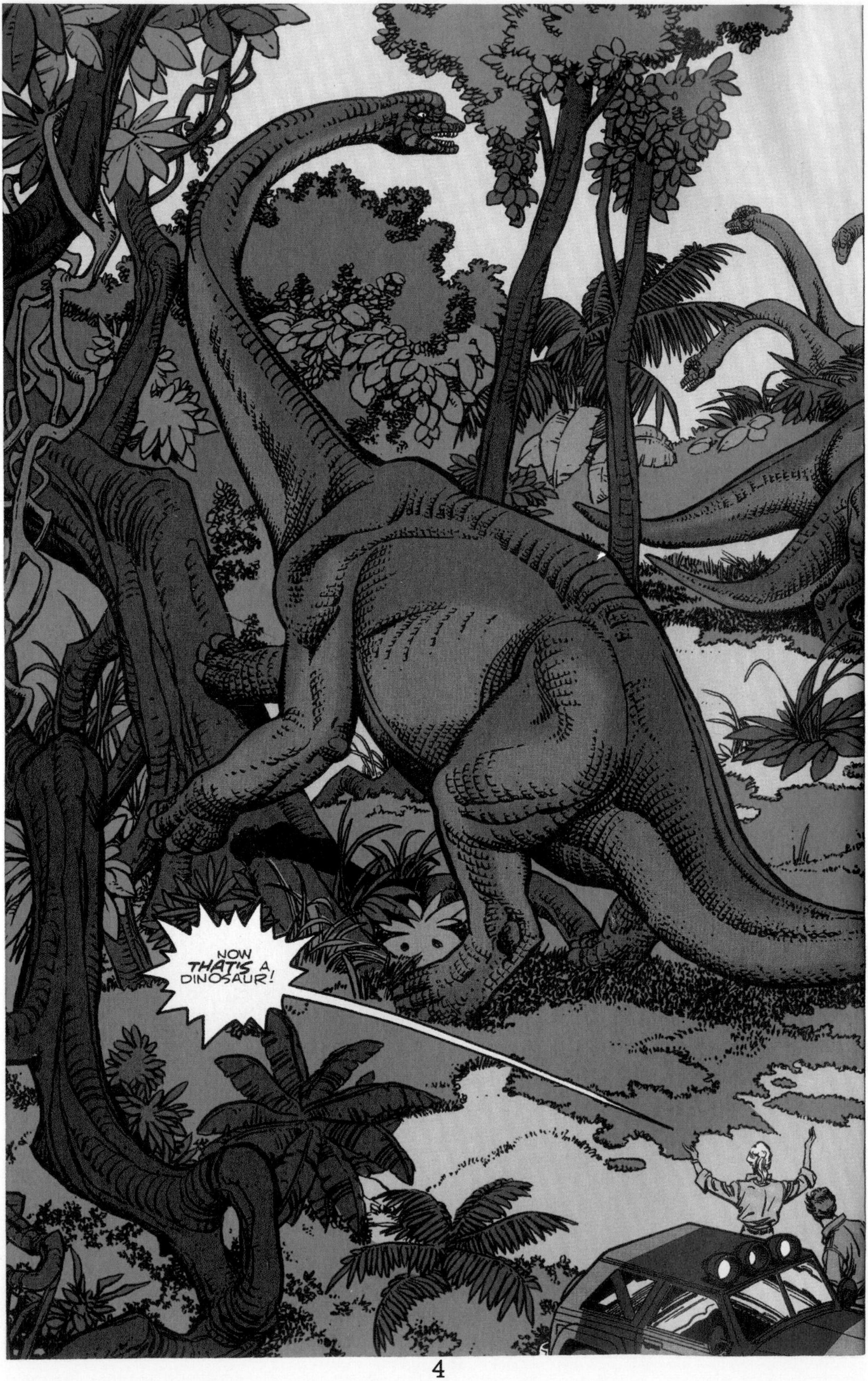
NOW THAT'S A DINOSAUR!

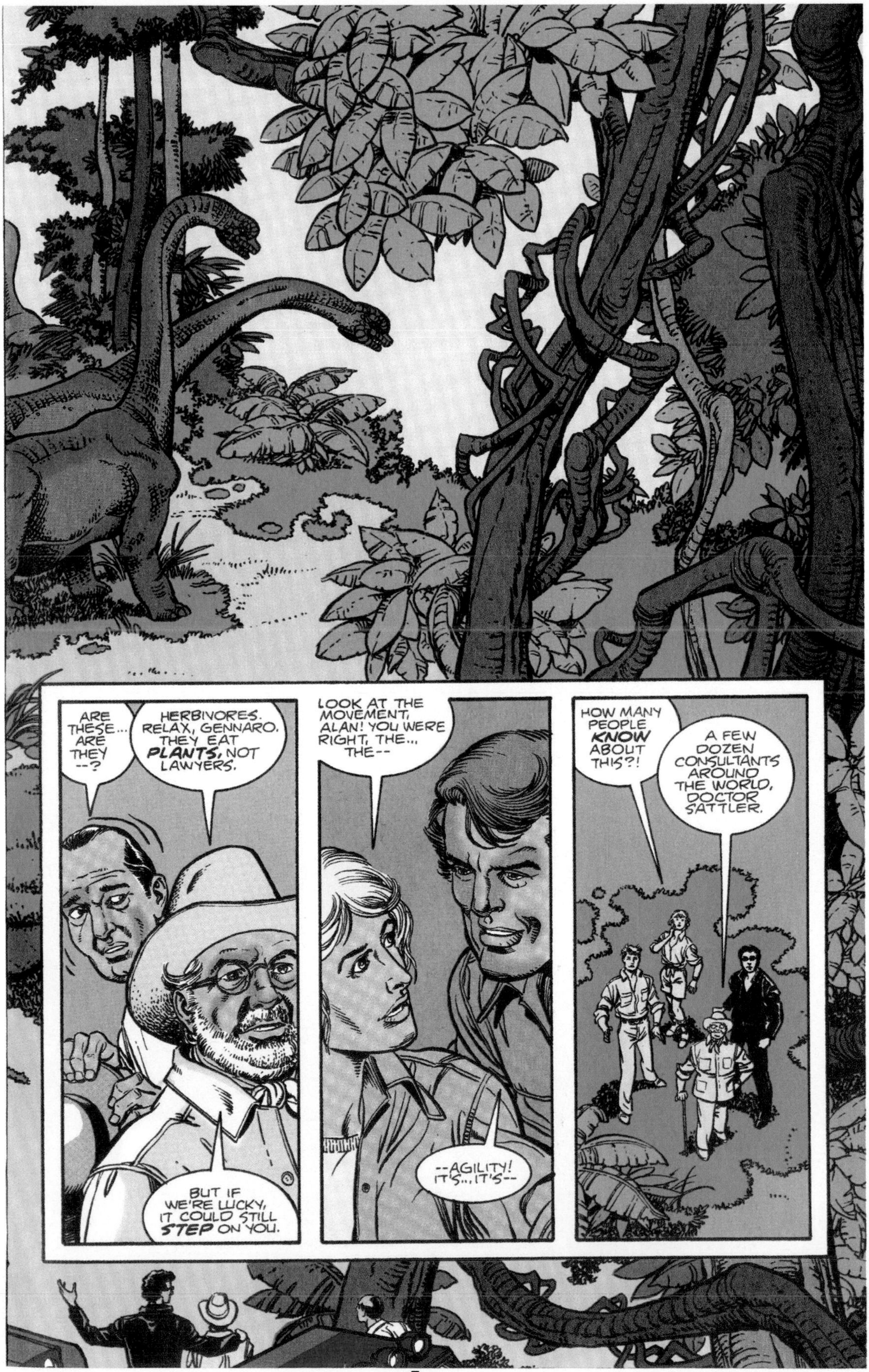

ARE THESE... ARE THEY --?
HERBIVORES. RELAX, GENNARO. THEY EAT PLANTS, NOT LAWYERS.
BUT IF WE'RE LUCKY, IT COULD STILL STEP ON YOU.
LOOK AT THE MOVEMENT, ALAN! YOU WERE RIGHT, THE... THE--
--AGILITY! IT'S... IT'S--
HOW MANY PEOPLE KNOW ABOUT THIS?!
A FEW DOZEN CONSULTANTS AROUND THE WORLD, DOCTOR SATTLER.

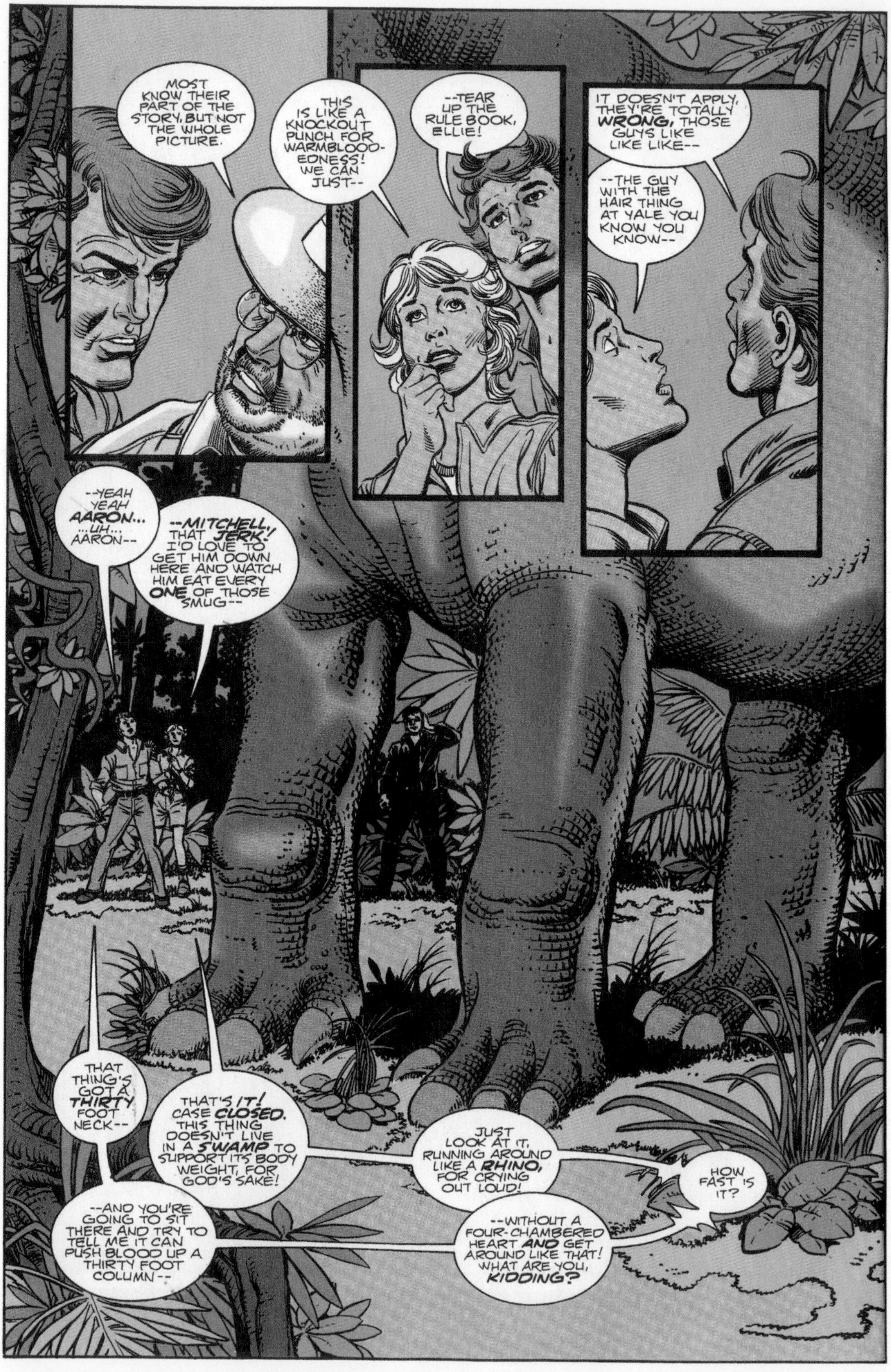
MOST KNOW THEIR PART OF THE STORY, BUT NOT THE WHOLE PICTURE.
THIS IS LIKE A KNOCKOUT PUNCH FOR WARMBLOODEDNESS! WE CAN JUST--
--TEAR UP THE RULE BOOK, ELLIE!
IT DOESN'T APPLY, THEY'RE TOTALLY WRONG, THOSE GUYS LIKE LIKE LIKE--
--THE GUY WITH THE HAIR THING AT YALE YOU KNOW YOU KNOW--
--YEAH YEAH AARON... ...UH... AARON--
--MITCHELL, THAT JERK! I'D LOVE TO GET HIM DOWN HERE AND WATCH HIM EAT EVERY ONE OF THOSE SMUG--
THAT THING'S GOT A THIRTY FOOT NECK--
--AND YOU'RE GOING TO SIT THERE AND TRY TO TELL ME IT CAN PUSH BLOOD UP A THIRTY FOOT COLUMN--
THAT'S IT! CASE CLOSED. THIS THING DOESN'T LIVE IN A SWAMP TO SUPPORT ITS BODY WEIGHT, FOR GOD'S SAKE!
JUST LOOK AT IT, RUNNING AROUND LIKE A RHINO, FOR CRYING OUT LOUD!
--WITHOUT A FOUR-CHAMBERED HEART AND GET AROUND LIKE THAT! WHAT ARE YOU, KIDDING?
HOW FAST IS IT?

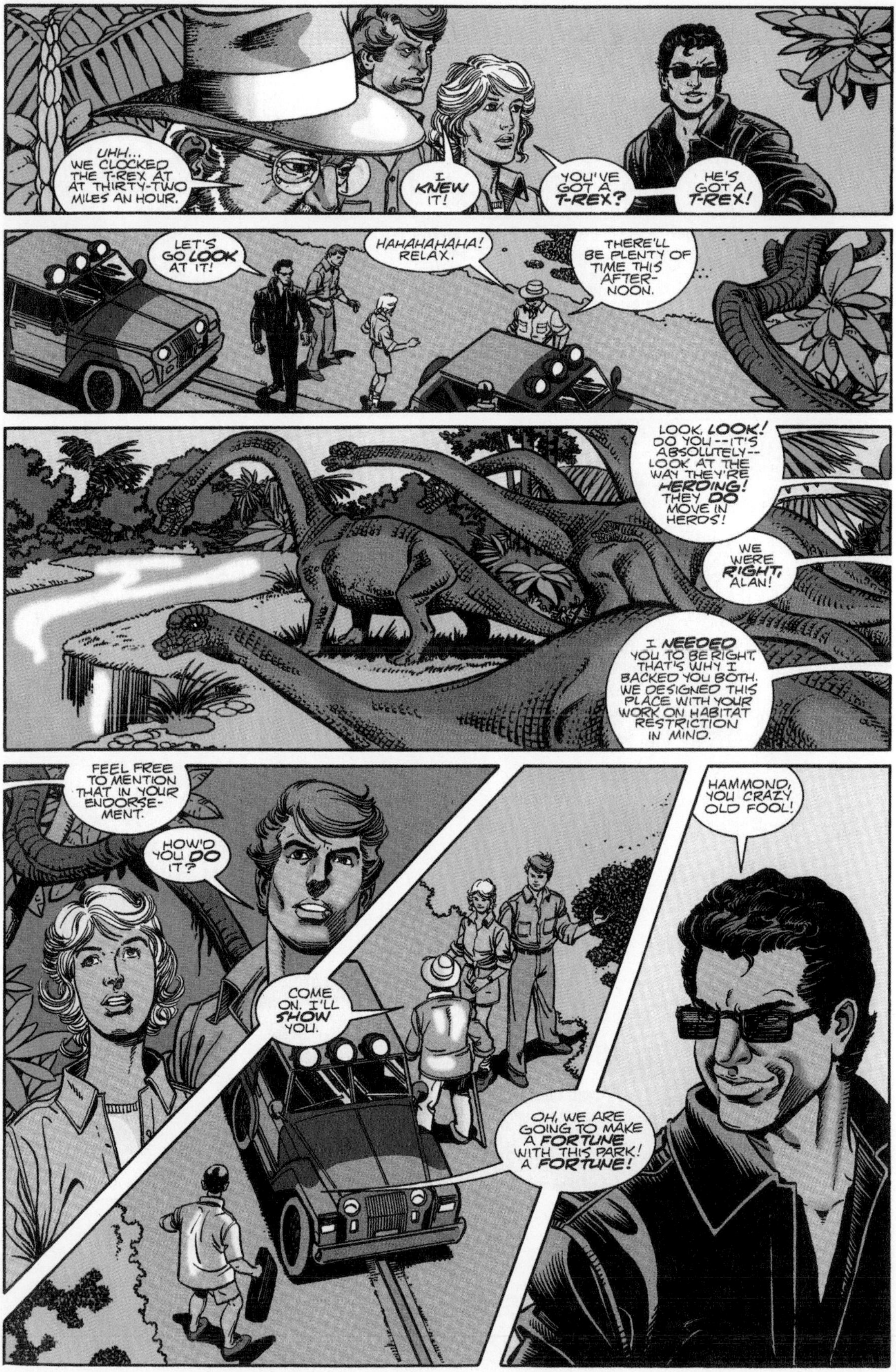
UHH... WE CLOCKED THE T-REX AT AT THIRTY-TWO MILES AN HOUR.
I KNEW IT!
YOU'VE GOT A T-REX?
HE'S GOT A T-REX!
LET'S GO LOOK AT IT!
HAHAHAHAHA! RELAX.
THERE'LL BE PLENTY OF TIME THIS AFTER-NOON.
LOOK, LOOK! DO YOU--IT'S ABSOLUTELY--LOOK AT THE WAY THEY'RE HERDING! THEY DO MOVE IN HERDS!
WE WERE RIGHT, ALAN!
I NEEDED YOU TO BE RIGHT. THAT'S WHY I BACKED YOU BOTH. WE DESIGNED THIS PLACE WITH YOUR WORK ON HABITAT RESTRICTION IN MIND.
FEEL FREE TO MENTION THAT IN YOUR ENDORSE-MENT.
HOW'D YOU DO IT?
COME ON. I'LL SHOW YOU.
HAMMOND, YOU CRAZY OLD FOOL!
OH, WE ARE GOING TO MAKE A FORTUNE WITH THIS PARK! A FORTUNE!

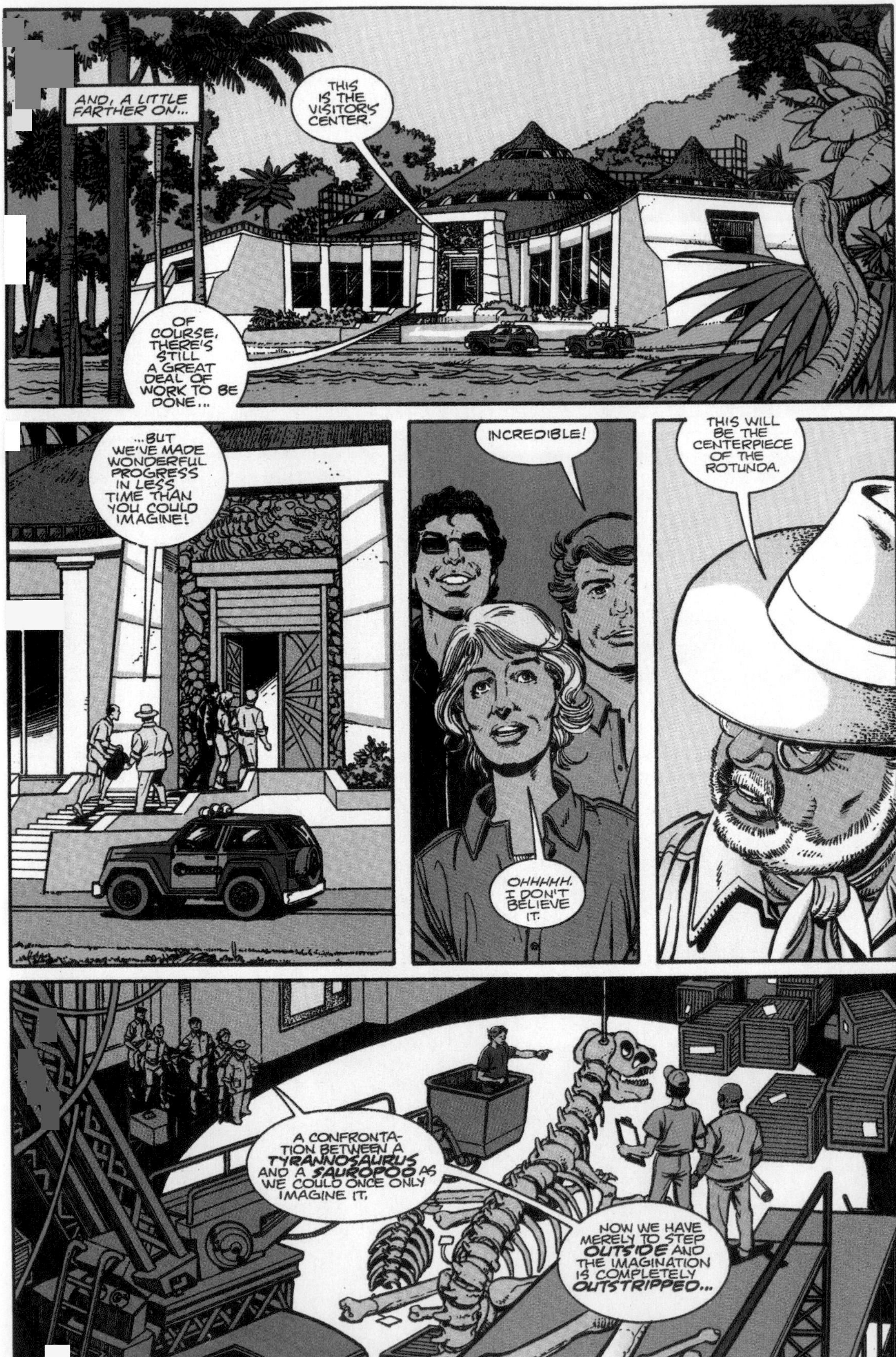
AND, A LITTLE FARTHER ON...
THIS IS THE VISITOR'S CENTER.
OF COURSE, THERE'S STILL A GREAT DEAL OF WORK TO BE DONE...
...BUT WE'VE MADE WONDERFUL PROGRESS IN LESS TIME THAN YOU COULD IMAGINE!
INCREDIBLE!
OHHHHH. I DON'T BELIEVE IT.
THIS WILL BE THE CENTERPIECE OF THE ROTUNDA.
A CONFRONTATION BETWEEN A TYRANNOSAURUS AND A SAUROPOD AS WE COULD ONCE ONLY IMAGINE IT.
NOW WE HAVE MERELY TO STEP OUTSIDE AND THE IMAGINATION IS COMPLETELY OUTSTRIPPED...

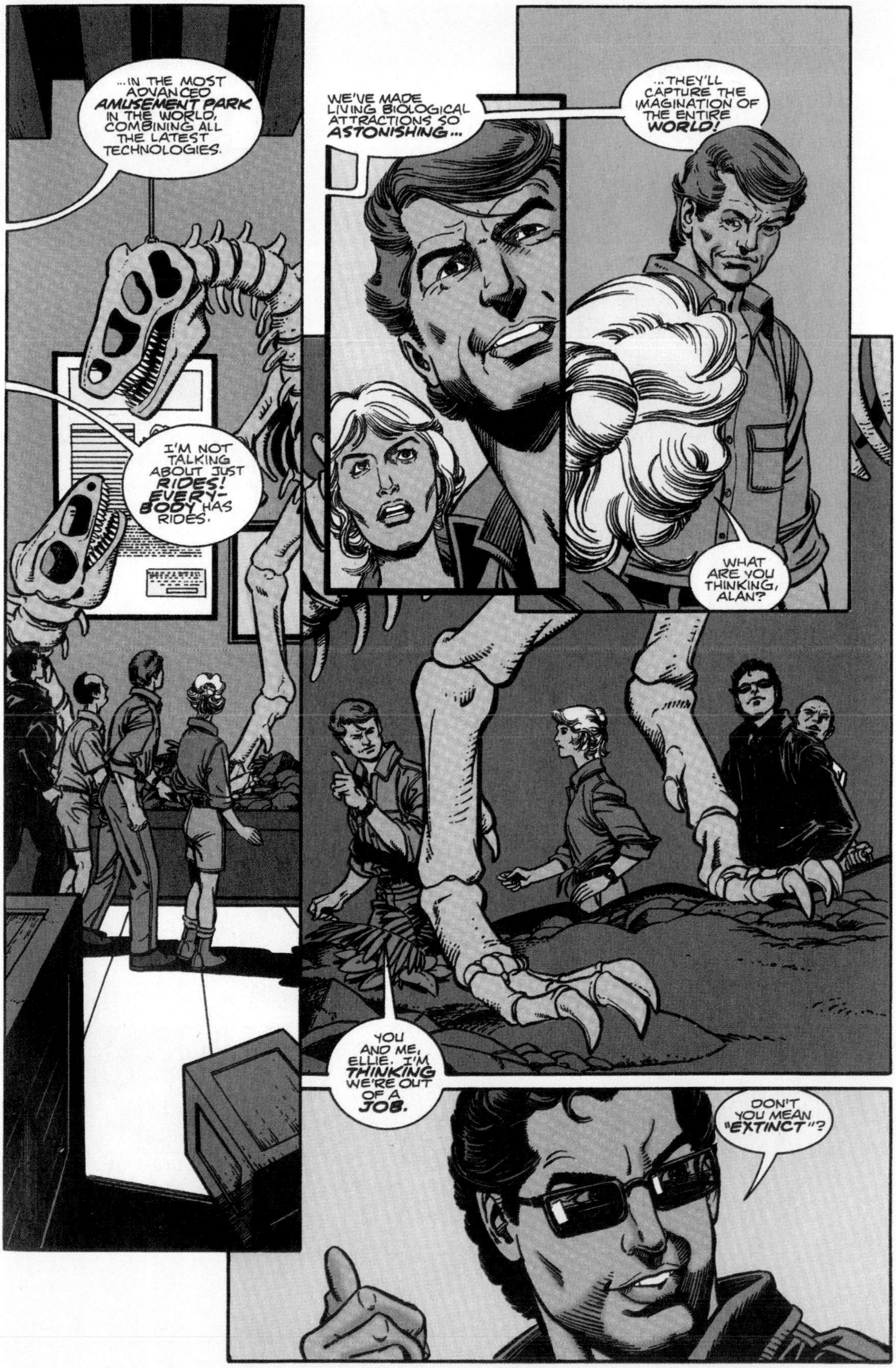

...IN THE MOST ADVANCED AMUSEMENT PARK IN THE WORLD, COMBINING ALL THE LATEST TECHNOLOGIES.
I'M NOT TALKING ABOUT JUST RIDES! EVERY-BODY HAS RIDES.
WE'VE MADE LIVING BIOLOGICAL ATTRACTIONS SO ASTONISHING...
...THEY'LL CAPTURE THE IMAGINATION OF THE ENTIRE WORLD!
WHAT ARE YOU THINKING, ALAN?
YOU AND ME, ELLIE. I'M THINKING WE'RE OUT OF A JOB.
DON'T YOU MEAN "EXTINCT"?

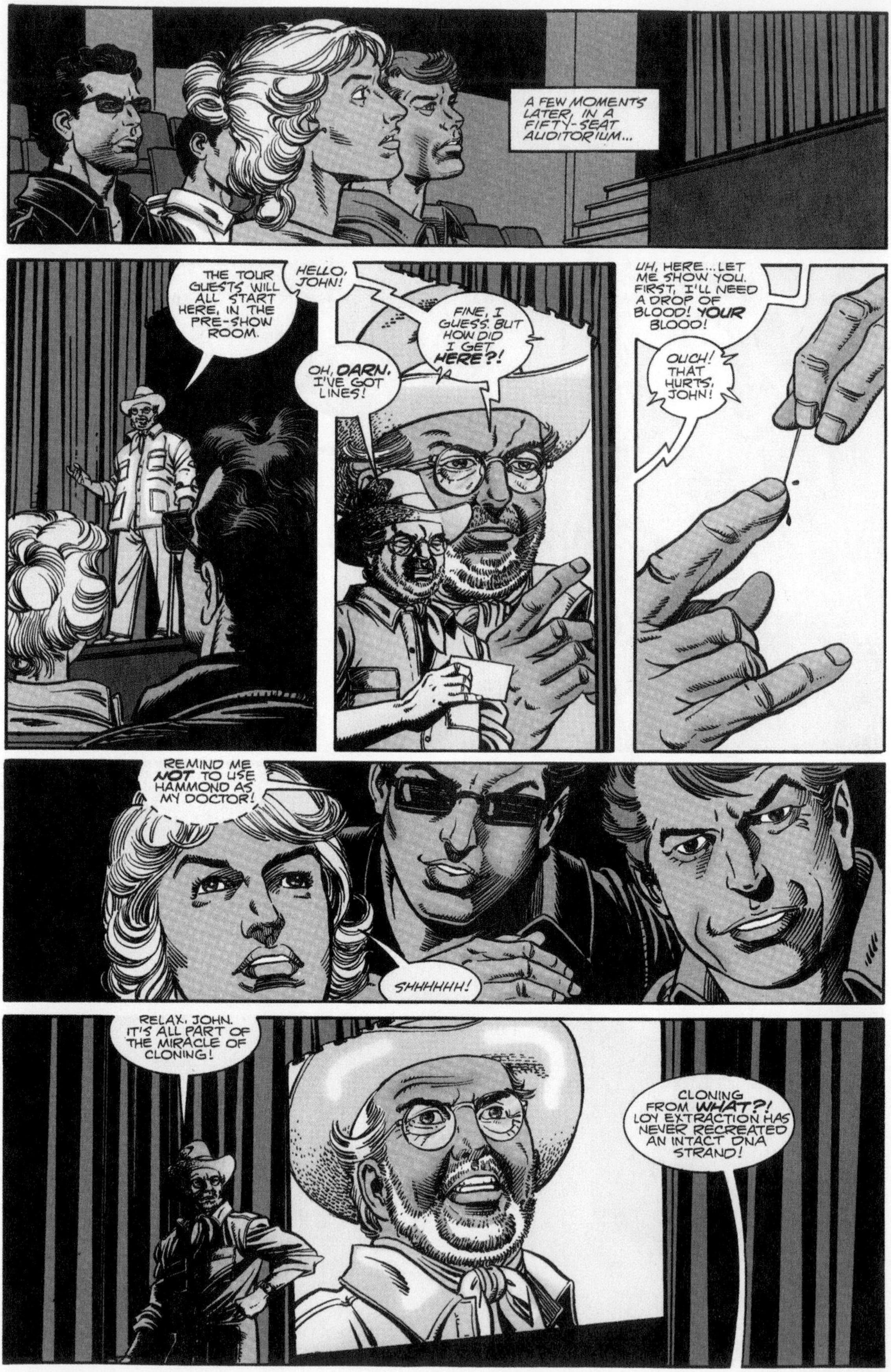
A FEW MOMENTS LATER, IN A FIFTY-SEAT AUDITORIUM...
THE TOUR GUESTS WILL ALL START HERE, IN THE PRE-SHOW ROOM.
HELLO, JOHN!
FINE, I GUESS. BUT HOW DID I GET HERE?!
OH, DARN. I'VE GOT LINES!
UH, HERE... LET ME SHOW YOU. FIRST, I'LL NEED A DROP OF BLOOD! YOUR BLOOD!
OUCH! THAT HURTS, JOHN!
REMIND ME NOT TO USE HAMMOND AS MY DOCTOR!
SHHHHHH!
RELAX, JOHN. IT'S ALL PART OF THE MIRACLE OF CLONING!
CLONING FROM WHAT?! LOY EXTRACTION HAS NEVER RECREATED AN INTACT DNA STRAND!

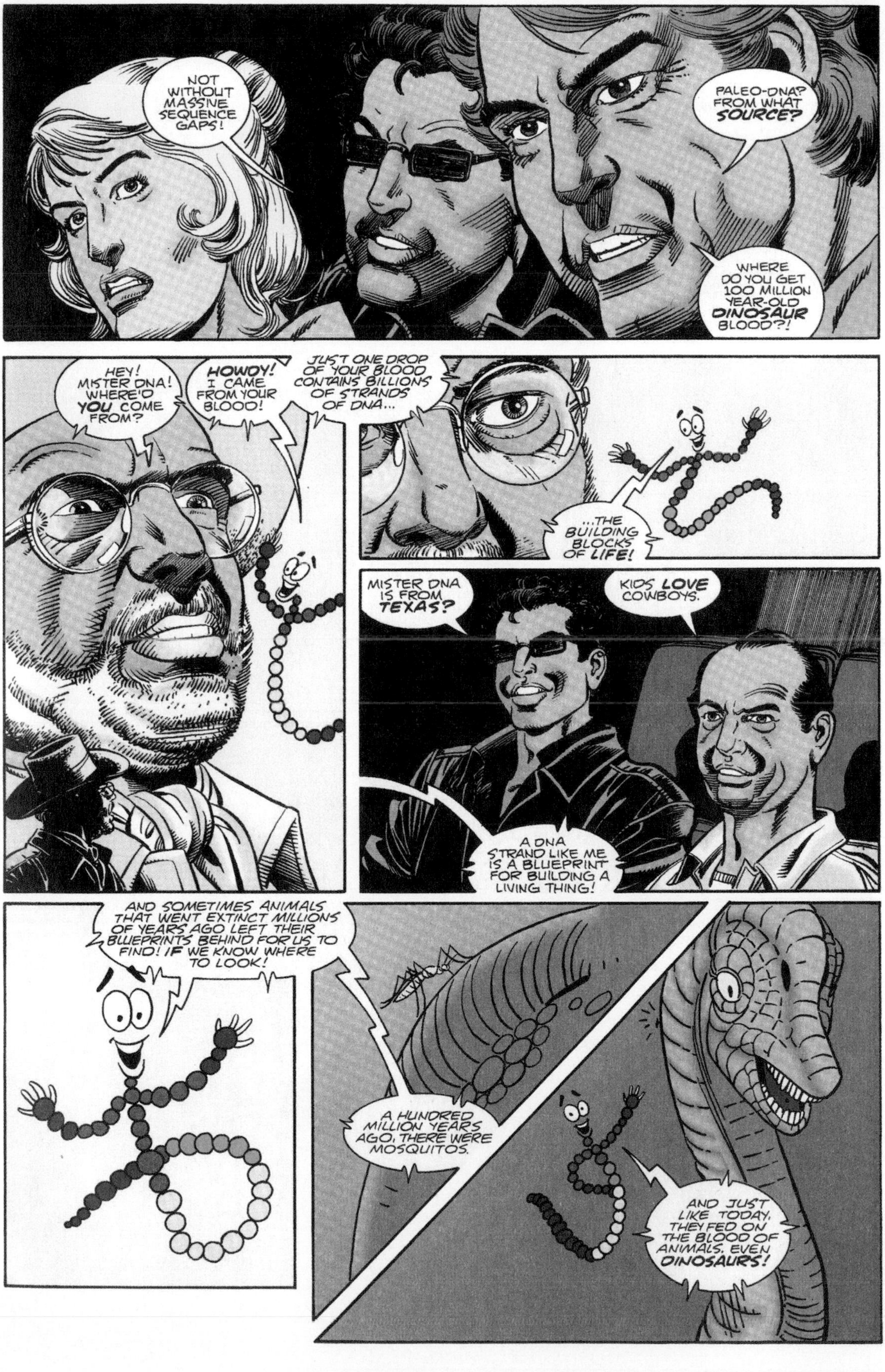
NOT WITHOUT MASSIVE SEQUENCE GAPS!
PALEO-DNA? FROM WHAT **SOURCE?**
WHERE DO YOU GET 100 MILLION YEAR-OLD **DINOSAUR** BLOOD?!
HEY! MISTER DNA! WHERE'D **YOU** COME FROM?
HOWDY! I CAME FROM YOUR BLOOD!
JUST ONE DROP OF YOUR BLOOD CONTAINS BILLIONS OF STRANDS OF DNA...
...THE BUILDING BLOCKS OF **LIFE!**
MISTER DNA IS FROM **TEXAS?**
KIDS **LOVE** COWBOYS.
A DNA STRAND LIKE ME IS A BLUEPRINT FOR BUILDING A LIVING THING!
AND SOMETIMES ANIMALS THAT WENT EXTINCT MILLIONS OF YEARS AGO LEFT THEIR BLUEPRINTS BEHIND FOR US TO FIND! **IF** WE KNOW WHERE TO LOOK!
A HUNDRED MILLION YEARS AGO, THERE WERE MOSQUITOS.
AND JUST LIKE TODAY, THEY FED ON THE BLOOD OF ANIMALS. EVEN **DINOSAURS!**

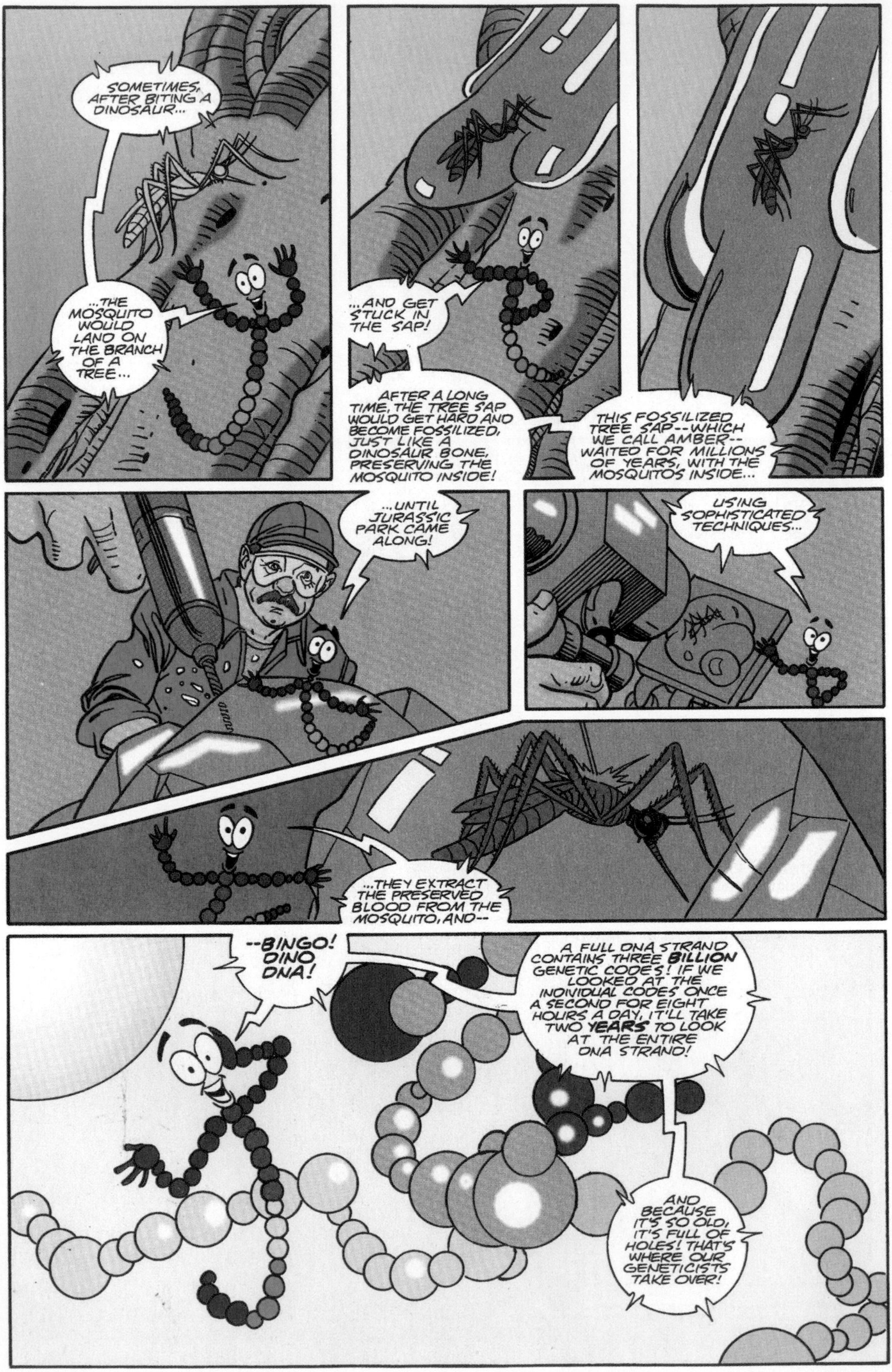
SOMETIMES, AFTER BITING A DINOSAUR...
...THE MOSQUITO WOULD LAND ON THE BRANCH OF A TREE...
...AND GET STUCK IN THE SAP!
AFTER A LONG TIME, THE TREE SAP WOULD GET HARD AND BECOME FOSSILIZED, JUST LIKE A DINOSAUR BONE, PRESERVING THE MOSQUITO INSIDE!
THIS FOSSILIZED TREE SAP--WHICH WE CALL AMBER--WAITED FOR MILLIONS OF YEARS, WITH THE MOSQUITOS INSIDE...
...UNTIL JURASSIC PARK CAME ALONG!
USING SOPHISTICATED TECHNIQUES...
...THEY EXTRACT THE PRESERVED BLOOD FROM THE MOSQUITO, AND--
--BINGO! DINO DNA!
A FULL DNA STRAND CONTAINS THREE BILLION GENETIC CODES! IF WE LOOKED AT THE INDIVIDUAL CODES ONCE A SECOND FOR EIGHT HOURS A DAY, IT'LL TAKE TWO YEARS TO LOOK AT THE ENTIRE DNA STRAND!
AND BECAUSE IT'S SO OLD, IT'S FULL OF HOLES! THAT'S WHERE OUR GENETICISTS TAKE OVER!

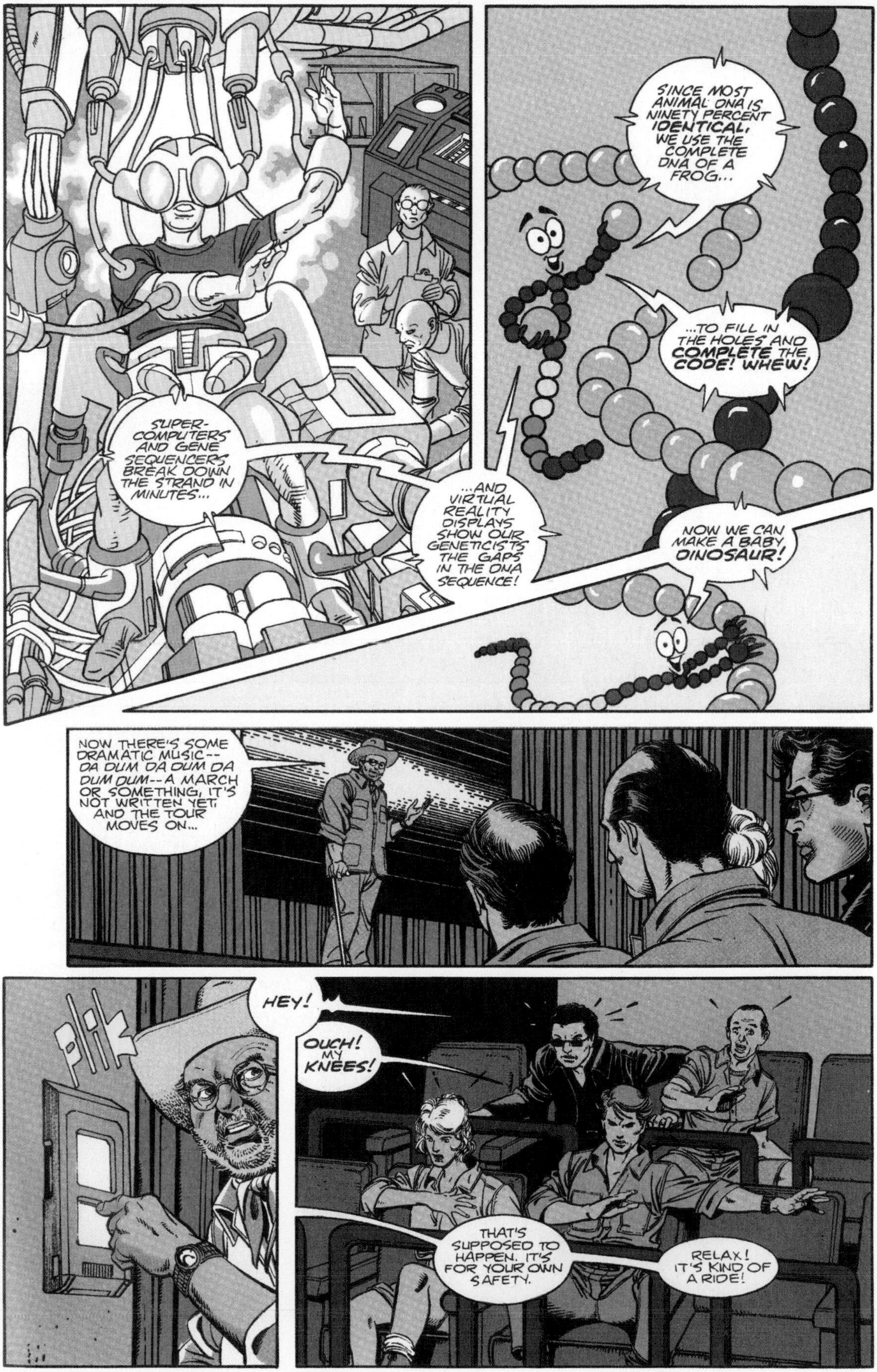
SINCE MOST ANIMAL DNA IS NINETY PERCENT IDENTICAL, WE USE THE COMPLETE DNA OF A FROG...
...TO FILL IN THE HOLES AND COMPLETE THE CODE! WHEW!
SUPER-COMPUTERS AND GENE SEQUENCERS BREAK DOWN THE STRAND IN MINUTES...
...AND VIRTUAL REALITY DISPLAYS SHOW OUR GENETICISTS THE GAPS IN THE DNA SEQUENCE!
NOW WE CAN MAKE A BABY DINOSAUR!
NOW THERE'S SOME DRAMATIC MUSIC-- DA DUM DA DUM DA DUM DUM--A MARCH OR SOMETHING, IT'S NOT WRITTEN YET. AND THE TOUR MOVES ON...
PLIK
HEY!
OUCH! MY KNEES!
THAT'S SUPPOSED TO HAPPEN. IT'S FOR YOUR OWN SAFETY.
RELAX! IT'S KIND OF A RIDE!

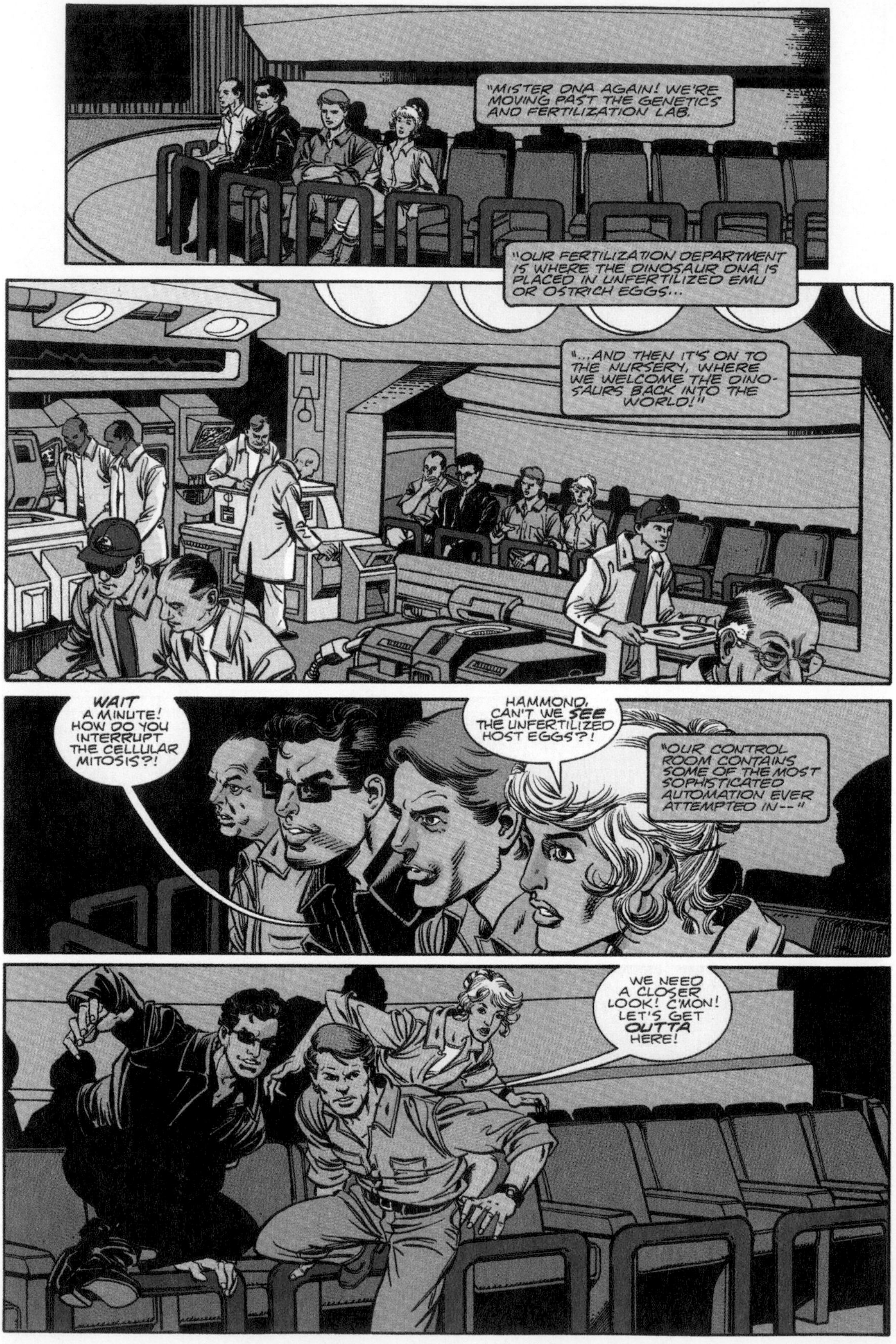
"MISTER DNA AGAIN! WE'RE MOVING PAST THE GENETICS AND FERTILIZATION LAB.
"OUR FERTILIZATION DEPARTMENT IS WHERE THE DINOSAUR DNA IS PLACED IN UNFERTILIZED EMU OR OSTRICH EGGS...
"...AND THEN IT'S ON TO THE NURSERY, WHERE WE WELCOME THE DINOSAURS BACK INTO THE WORLD!"
WAIT A MINUTE! HOW DO YOU INTERRUPT THE CELLULAR MITOSIS?!
HAMMOND, CAN'T WE SEE THE UNFERTILIZED HOST EGGS?!
"OUR CONTROL ROOM CONTAINS SOME OF THE MOST SOPHISTICATED AUTOMATION EVER ATTEMPTED IN--"
WE NEED A CLOSER LOOK! C'MON! LET'S GET OUTTA HERE!

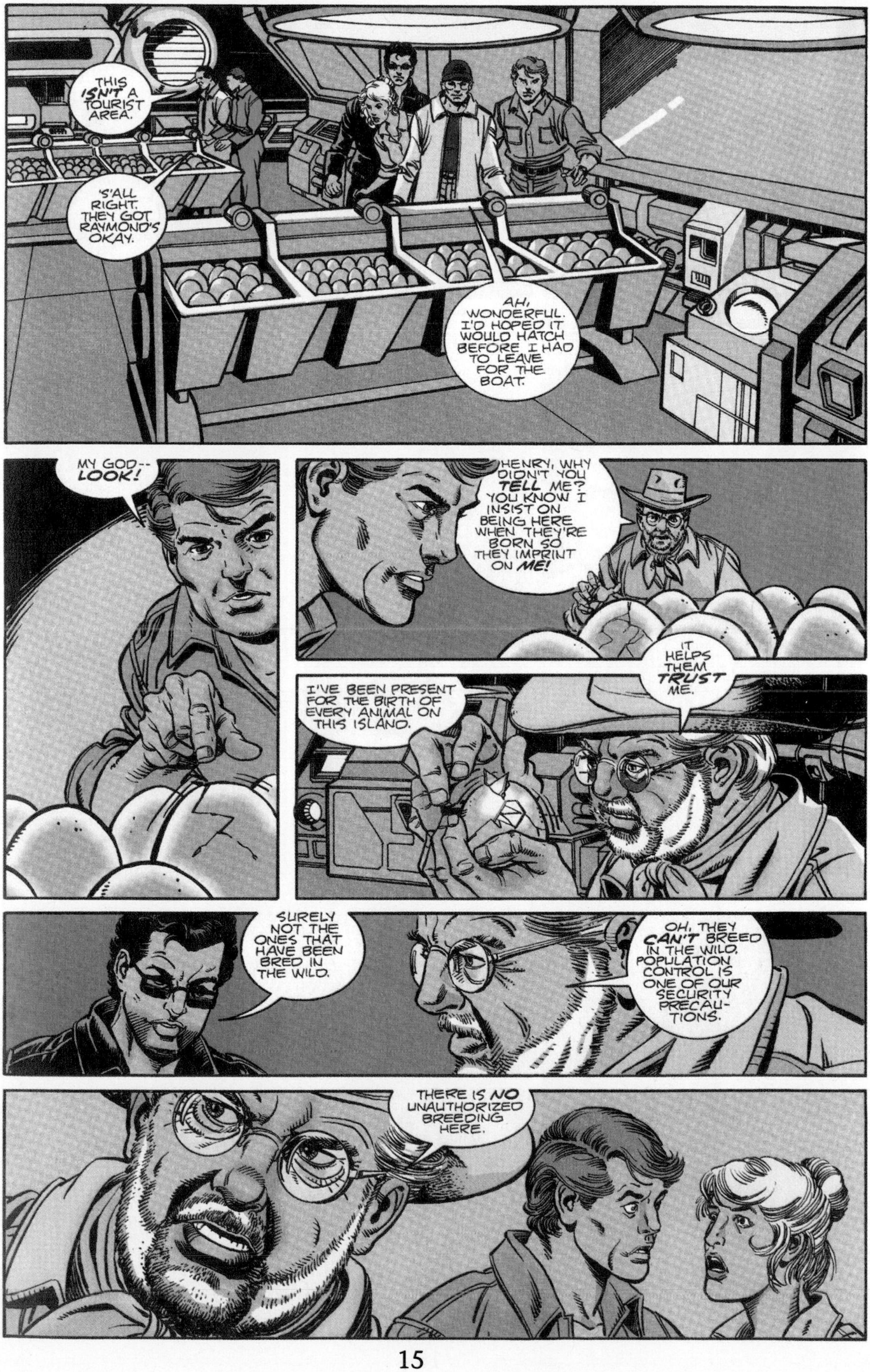
THIS ISN'T A TOURIST AREA.
'S'ALL RIGHT. THEY GOT RAYMOND'S OKAY.
AH, WONDERFUL. I'D HOPED IT WOULD HATCH BEFORE I HAD TO LEAVE FOR THE BOAT.
MY GOD-- LOOK!
HENRY, WHY DIDN'T YOU TELL ME? YOU KNOW I INSIST ON BEING HERE WHEN THEY'RE BORN SO THEY IMPRINT ON ME!
I'VE BEEN PRESENT FOR THE BIRTH OF EVERY ANIMAL ON THIS ISLAND.
IT HELPS THEM TRUST ME.
SURELY NOT THE ONES THAT HAVE BEEN BRED IN THE WILD.
OH, THEY CAN'T BREED IN THE WILD. POPULATION CONTROL IS ONE OF OUR SECURITY PRECAU- TIONS.
THERE IS NO UNAUTHORIZED BREEDING HERE.

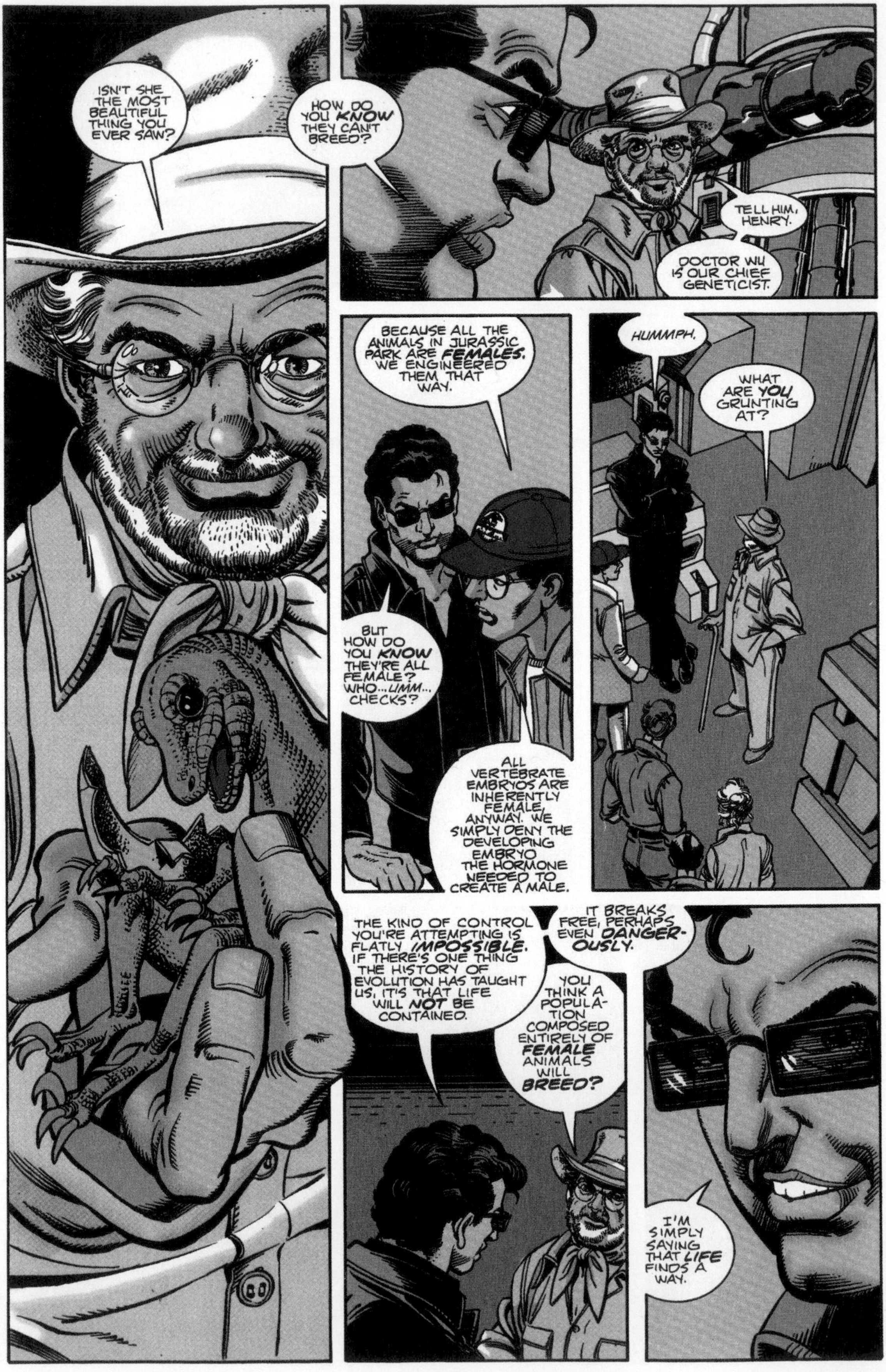
ISN'T SHE THE MOST BEAUTIFUL THING YOU EVER SAW?
HOW DO YOU KNOW THEY CAN'T BREED?
TELL HIM, HENRY.
DOCTOR WU IS OUR CHIEF GENETICIST.
BECAUSE ALL THE ANIMALS IN JURASSIC PARK ARE FEMALES. WE ENGINEERED THEM THAT WAY.
BUT HOW DO YOU KNOW THEY'RE ALL FEMALE? WHO...UMM... CHECKS?
ALL VERTEBRATE EMBRYOS ARE INHERENTLY FEMALE, ANYWAY. WE SIMPLY DENY THE DEVELOPING EMBRYO THE HORMONE NEEDED TO CREATE A MALE.
HUMMPH.
WHAT ARE YOU GRUNTING AT?
THE KIND OF CONTROL YOU'RE ATTEMPTING IS FLATLY IMPOSSIBLE. IF THERE'S ONE THING THE HISTORY OF EVOLUTION HAS TAUGHT US, IT'S THAT LIFE WILL NOT BE CONTAINED.
IT BREAKS FREE, PERHAPS EVEN DANGEROUSLY.
YOU THINK A POPULATION COMPOSED ENTIRELY OF FEMALE ANIMALS WILL BREED?
I'M SIMPLY SAYING THAT LIFE FINDS A WAY.

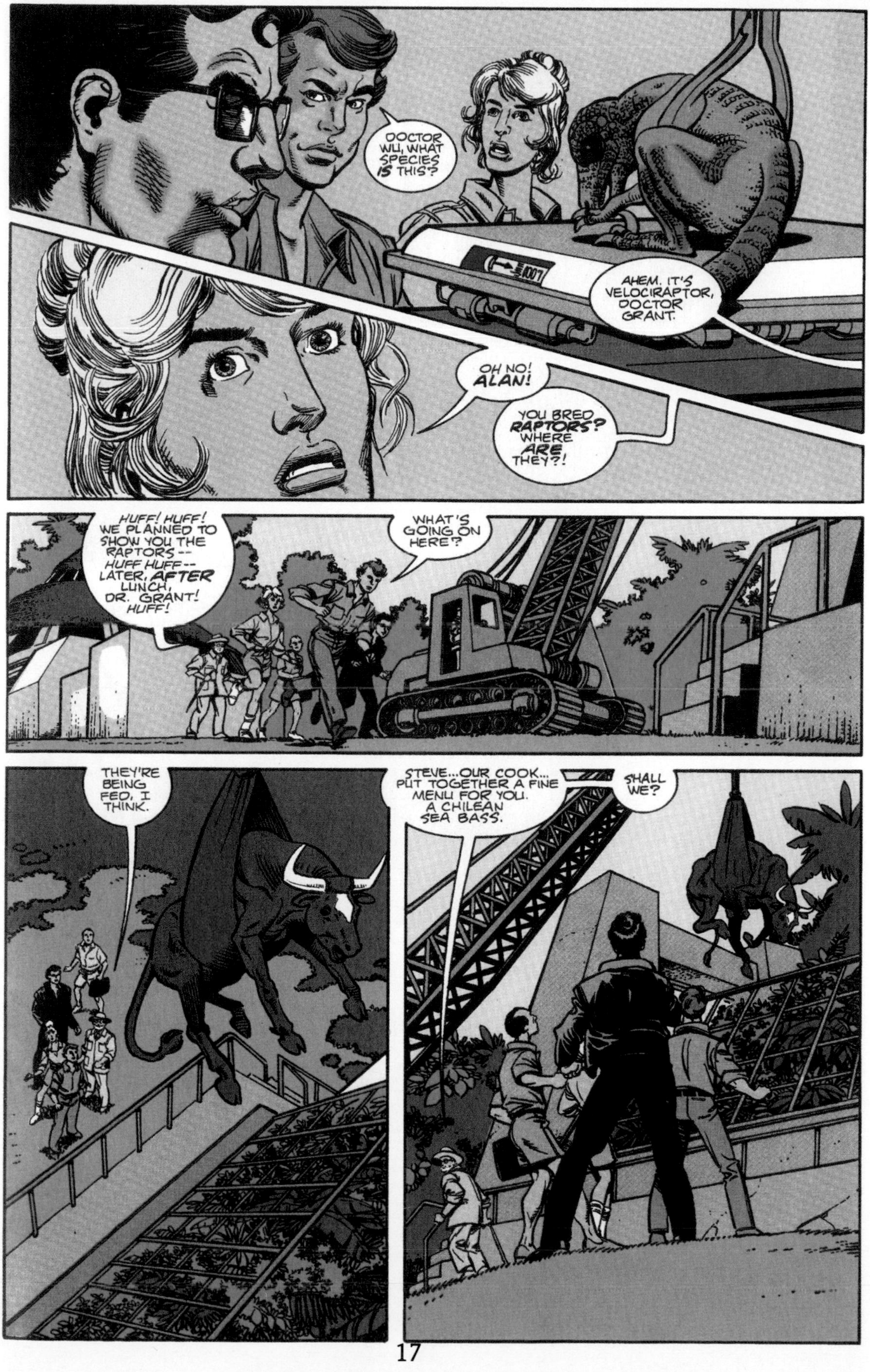
DOCTOR WU, WHAT SPECIES IS THIS?
AHEM. IT'S VELOCIRAPTOR, DOCTOR GRANT.
OH NO! ALAN!
YOU BRED RAPTORS? WHERE ARE THEY?!
HUFF! HUFF! WE PLANNED TO SHOW YOU THE RAPTORS-- HUFF HUFF-- LATER, AFTER LUNCH, DR. GRANT! HUFF!
WHAT'S GOING ON HERE?
THEY'RE BEING FED, I THINK.
STEVE...OUR COOK... PUT TOGETHER A FINE MENU FOR YOU. A CHILEAN SEA BASS.
SHALL WE?

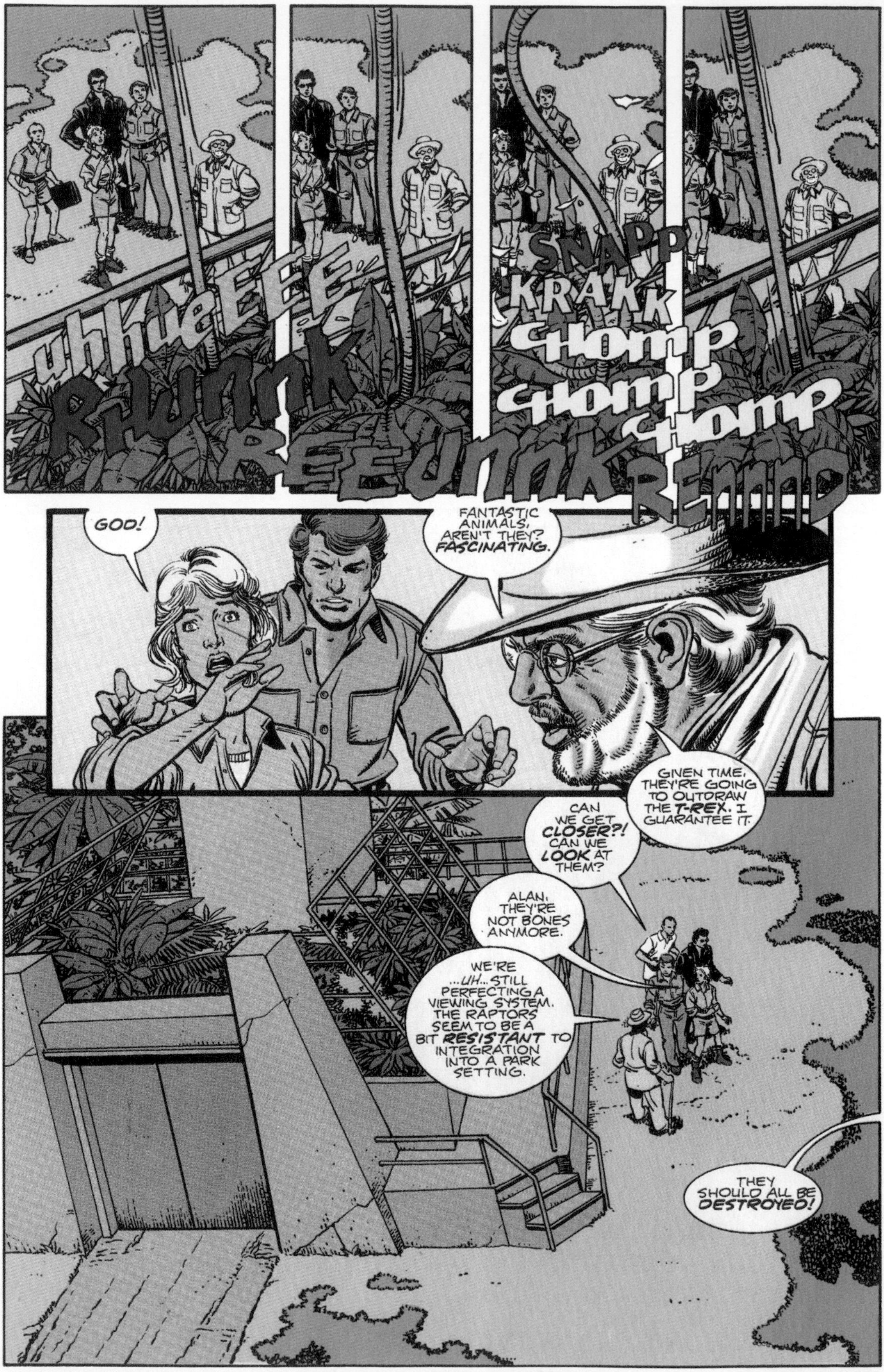
uhhueEEE
RWUNNK
REEEUNNK
SNAPP
KRAKK
CHOMP
CHOMP
CHOMP
RENNND
GOD!
FANTASTIC ANIMALS, AREN'T THEY? FASCINATING.
GIVEN TIME, THEY'RE GOING TO OUTDRAW THE T-REX. I GUARANTEE IT.
CAN WE GET CLOSER?! CAN WE LOOK AT THEM?
ALAN, THEY'RE NOT BONES ANYMORE.
WE'RE ...UH... STILL PERFECTING A VIEWING SYSTEM. THE RAPTORS SEEM TO BE A BIT RESISTANT TO INTEGRATION INTO A PARK SETTING.
THEY SHOULD ALL BE DESTROYED!

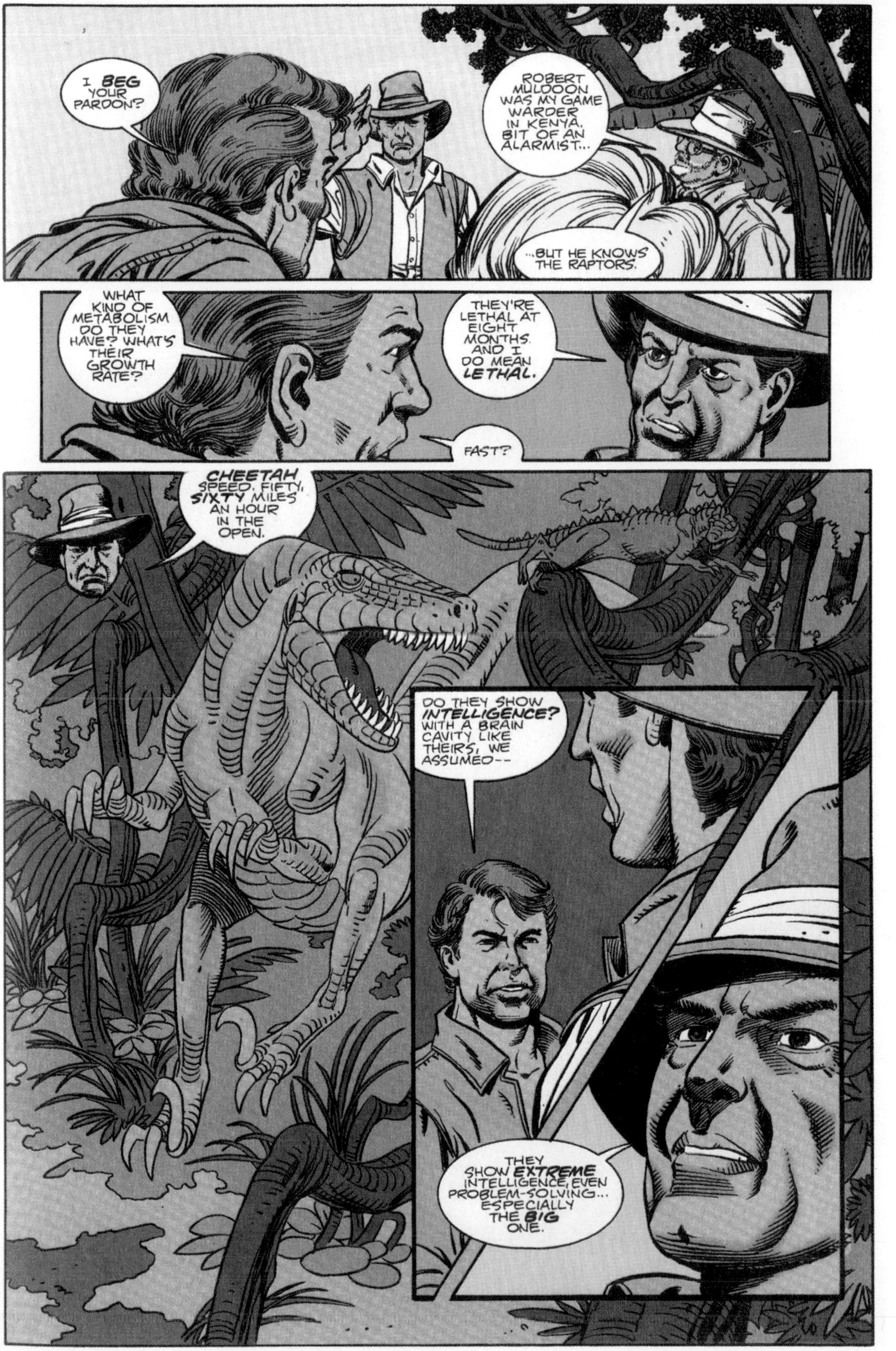
I BEG YOUR PARDON?
ROBERT MULDOON WAS MY GAME WARDER IN KENYA, BIT OF AN ALARMIST...
...BUT HE KNOWS THE RAPTORS.
WHAT KIND OF METABOLISM DO THEY HAVE? WHAT'S THEIR GROWTH RATE?
THEY'RE LETHAL AT EIGHT MONTHS. AND I DO MEAN LETHAL.
FAST?
CHEETAH SPEED. FIFTY, SIXTY MILES AN HOUR IN THE OPEN.
DO THEY SHOW INTELLIGENCE? WITH A BRAIN CAVITY LIKE THEIRS, WE ASSUMED--
THEY SHOW EXTREME INTELLIGENCE, EVEN PROBLEM-SOLVING... ESPECIALLY THE BIG ONE.

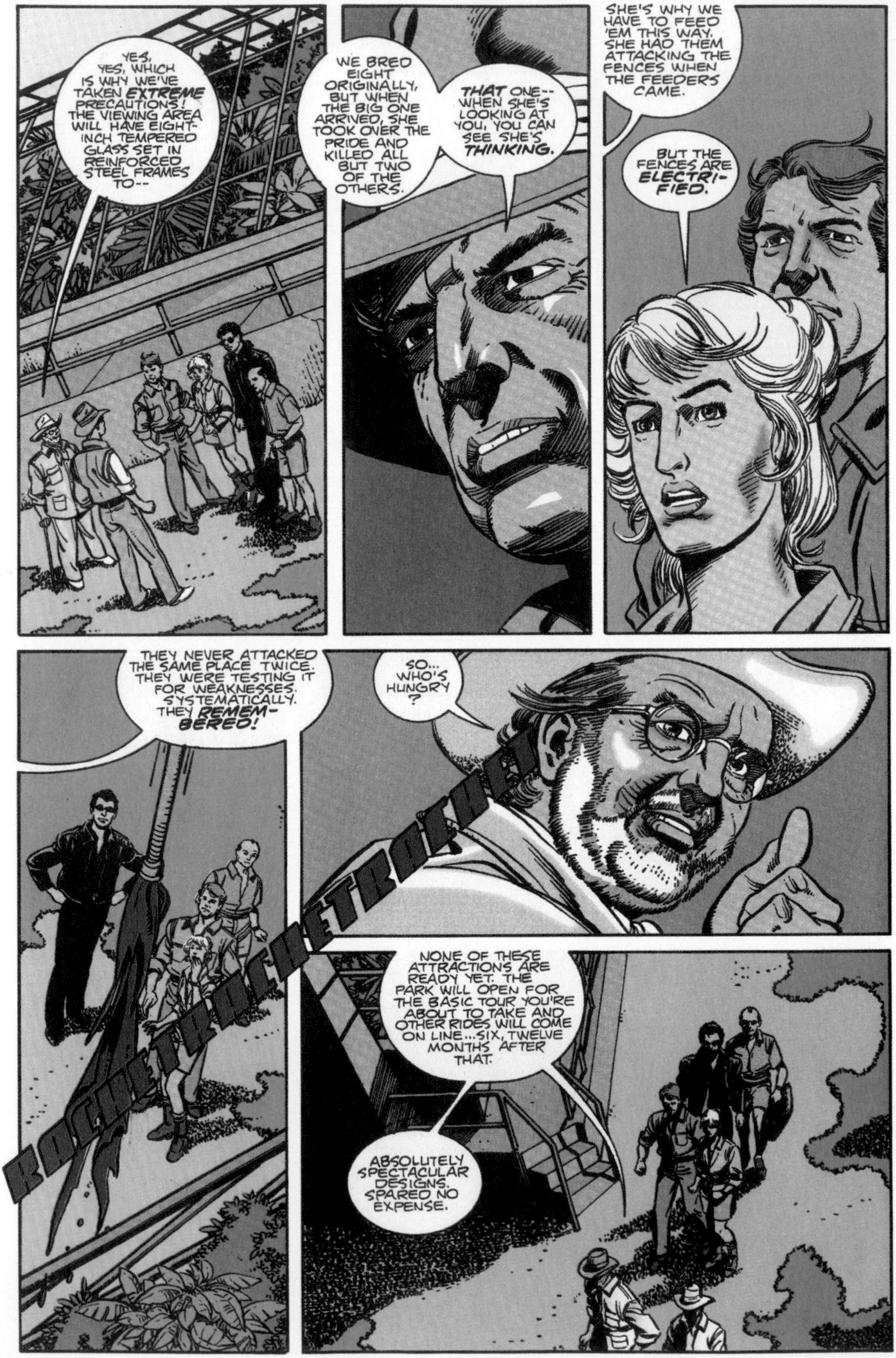
YES, YES, WHICH IS WHY WE'VE TAKEN EXTREME PRECAUTIONS! THE VIEWING AREA WILL HAVE EIGHT-INCH TEMPERED GLASS SET IN REINFORCED STEEL FRAMES TO--
WE BRED EIGHT ORIGINALLY, BUT WHEN THE BIG ONE ARRIVED, SHE TOOK OVER THE PRIDE AND KILLED ALL BUT TWO OF THE OTHERS.
THAT ONE-- WHEN SHE'S LOOKING AT YOU, YOU CAN SEE SHE'S THINKING.
SHE'S WHY WE HAVE TO FEED 'EM THIS WAY. SHE HAD THEM ATTACKING THE FENCES WHEN THE FEEDERS CAME.
BUT THE FENCES ARE ELECTRI-FIED.
THEY NEVER ATTACKED THE SAME PLACE TWICE. THEY WERE TESTING IT FOR WEAKNESSES. SYSTEMATICALLY. THEY REMEM-BERED!
SO... WHO'S HUNGRY?
RACHETRACHETRACHET
NONE OF THESE ATTRACTIONS ARE READY YET. THE PARK WILL OPEN FOR THE BASIC TOUR YOU'RE ABOUT TO TAKE AND OTHER RIDES WILL COME ON LINE...SIX, TWELVE MONTHS AFTER THAT.
ABSOLUTELY SPECTACULAR DESIGNS. SPARED NO EXPENSE.

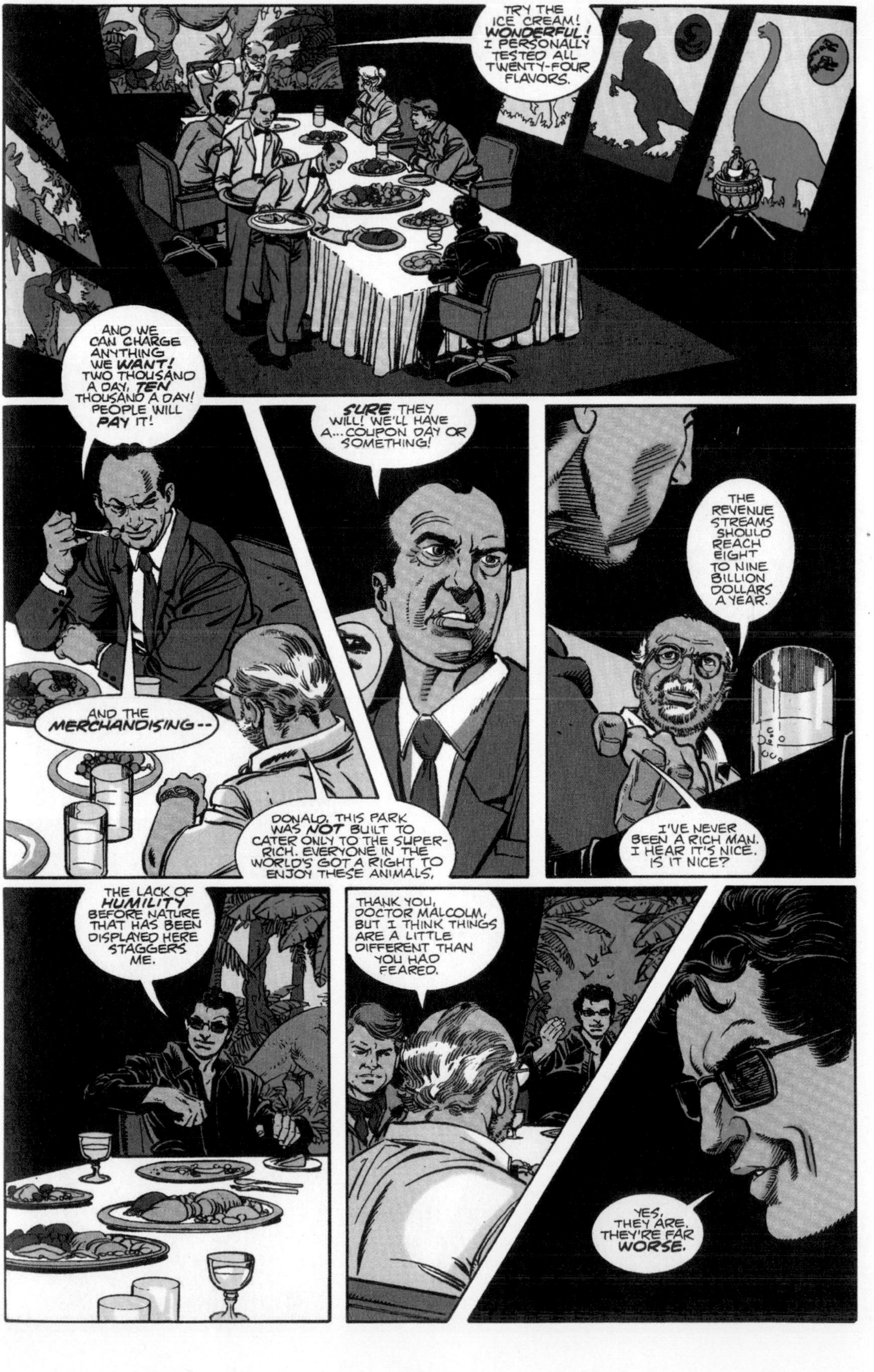
TRY THE ICE CREAM! WONDERFUL! I PERSONALLY TESTED ALL TWENTY-FOUR FLAVORS.
AND WE CAN CHARGE ANYTHING WE WANT! TWO THOUSAND A DAY, TEN THOUSAND A DAY! PEOPLE WILL PAY IT!
AND THE MERCHANDISING--
DONALD, THIS PARK WAS NOT BUILT TO CATER ONLY TO THE SUPER-RICH. EVERYONE IN THE WORLD'S GOT A RIGHT TO ENJOY THESE ANIMALS.
SURE THEY WILL! WE'LL HAVE A...COUPON DAY OR SOMETHING!
THE REVENUE STREAMS SHOULD REACH EIGHT TO NINE BILLION DOLLARS A YEAR.
I'VE NEVER BEEN A RICH MAN. I HEAR IT'S NICE. IS IT NICE?
THE LACK OF HUMILITY BEFORE NATURE THAT HAS BEEN DISPLAYED HERE STAGGERS ME.
THANK YOU, DOCTOR MALCOLM, BUT I THINK THINGS ARE A LITTLE DIFFERENT THAN YOU HAD FEARED.
YES, THEY ARE. THEY'RE FAR WORSE.

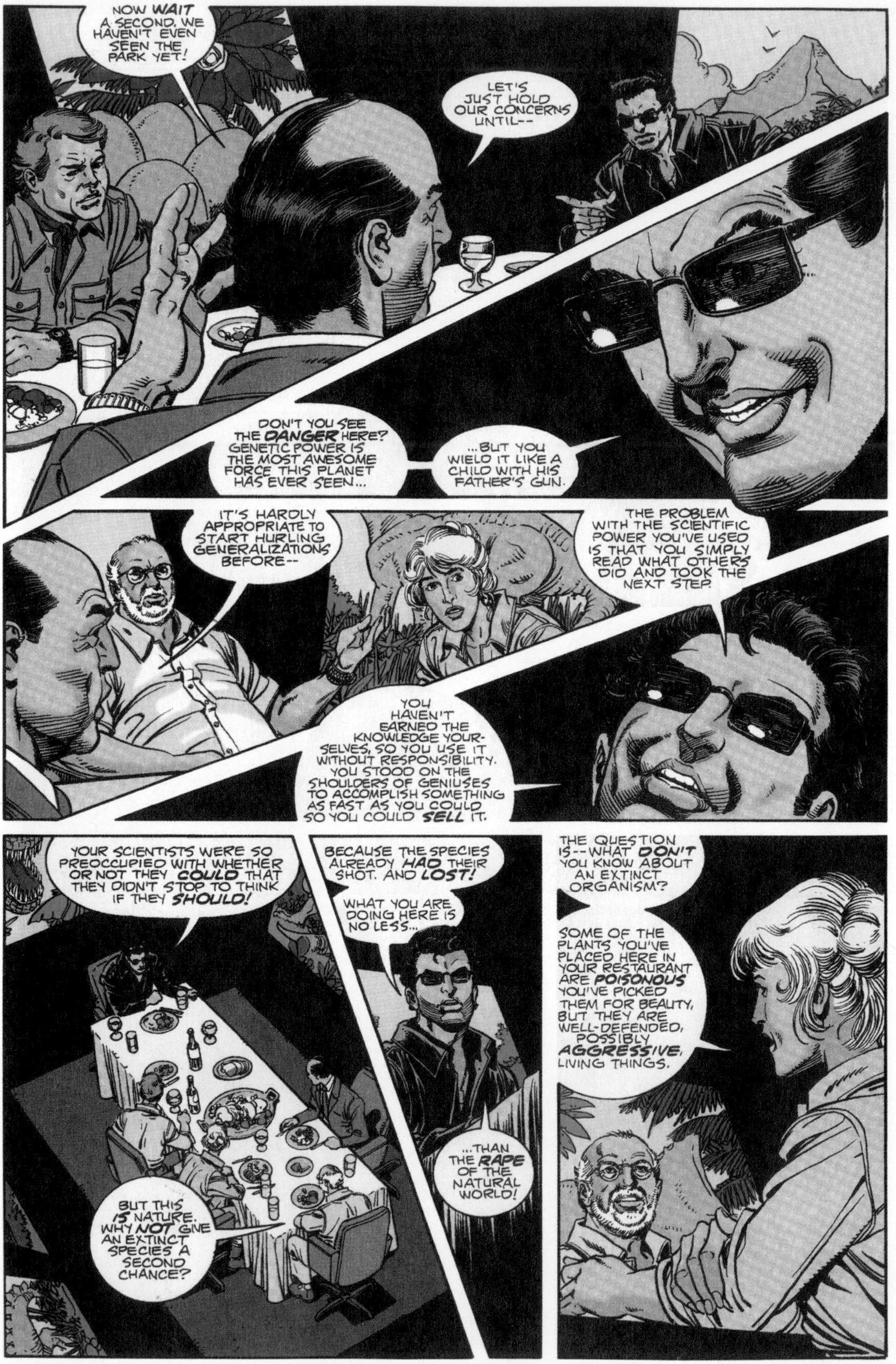
NOW WAIT A SECOND, WE HAVEN'T EVEN SEEN THE PARK YET!
LET'S JUST HOLD OUR CONCERNS UNTIL--
DON'T YOU SEE THE DANGER HERE? GENETIC POWER IS THE MOST AWESOME FORCE THIS PLANET HAS EVER SEEN...
...BUT YOU WIELD IT LIKE A CHILD WITH HIS FATHER'S GUN.
IT'S HARDLY APPROPRIATE TO START HURLING GENERALIZATIONS BEFORE--
THE PROBLEM WITH THE SCIENTIFIC POWER YOU'VE USED IS THAT YOU SIMPLY READ WHAT OTHERS DID AND TOOK THE NEXT STEP.
YOU HAVEN'T EARNED THE KNOWLEDGE YOURSELVES, SO YOU USE IT WITHOUT RESPONSIBILITY. YOU STOOD ON THE SHOULDERS OF GENIUSES TO ACCOMPLISH SOMETHING AS FAST AS YOU COULD SO YOU COULD SELL IT.
YOUR SCIENTISTS WERE SO PREOCCUPIED WITH WHETHER OR NOT THEY COULD THAT THEY DIDN'T STOP TO THINK IF THEY SHOULD!
BUT THIS IS NATURE. WHY NOT GIVE AN EXTINCT SPECIES A SECOND CHANCE?
BECAUSE THE SPECIES ALREADY HAD THEIR SHOT. AND LOST!
WHAT YOU ARE DOING HERE IS NO LESS...
...THAN THE RAPE OF THE NATURAL WORLD!
THE QUESTION IS--WHAT DON'T YOU KNOW ABOUT AN EXTINCT ORGANISM?
SOME OF THE PLANTS YOU'VE PLACED HERE IN YOUR RESTAURANT ARE POISONOUS. YOU'VE PICKED THEM FOR BEAUTY, BUT THEY ARE WELL-DEFENDED, POSSIBLY AGGRESSIVE, LIVING THINGS.

DOCTOR GRANT, IF THERE'S ONE PERSON WHO CAN APPRECIATE ALL THIS--

I FEEL... ELATED...AND FRIGHTENED AND...

THE WORLD HAS JUST CHANGED RADICALLY.

DINOSAURS AND MAN, SEPARATED BY 65 MILLION YEARS OF EVOLUTION HAVE BEEN SUDDENLY THROWN INTO THE MIX TOGETHER.

HOW CAN WE HAVE THE FAINTEST IDEA WHAT TO EXPECT?

I EXPECTED YOU TO DEFEND *AGAINST* THESE GUYS AND THE ONLY ONE I'VE GOT ON MY SIDE IS THE BLOOD-SUCKING *LAWYER?*

OH, THANKS JOHN.

SUDDENLY, FROM OUTSIDE... THE SOUND OF A HORN HONKING...

AH... TIM AND ALEXIS ARE HERE.

WHO?

YOU FOUR ARE GOING TO HAVE A LITTLE COMPANY OUT IN THE PARK. SPEND A LITTLE TIME WITH OUR TARGET AUDIENCE.

GRANDPA!

MAYBE THEY'LL HELP YOU GET INTO THE SPIRIT OF THE PLACE.

KIDS?

HAVE A HEART, GENTLEMEN. THEIR PARENTS ARE GETTING A DIVORCE AND THEY NEED A DIVERSION.

HI, DOCTOR GRANT. I READ YOUR BOOK!

OH, THAT'S ...UH... GREAT.

HELLO, LEX. I'M ELLIE.

23

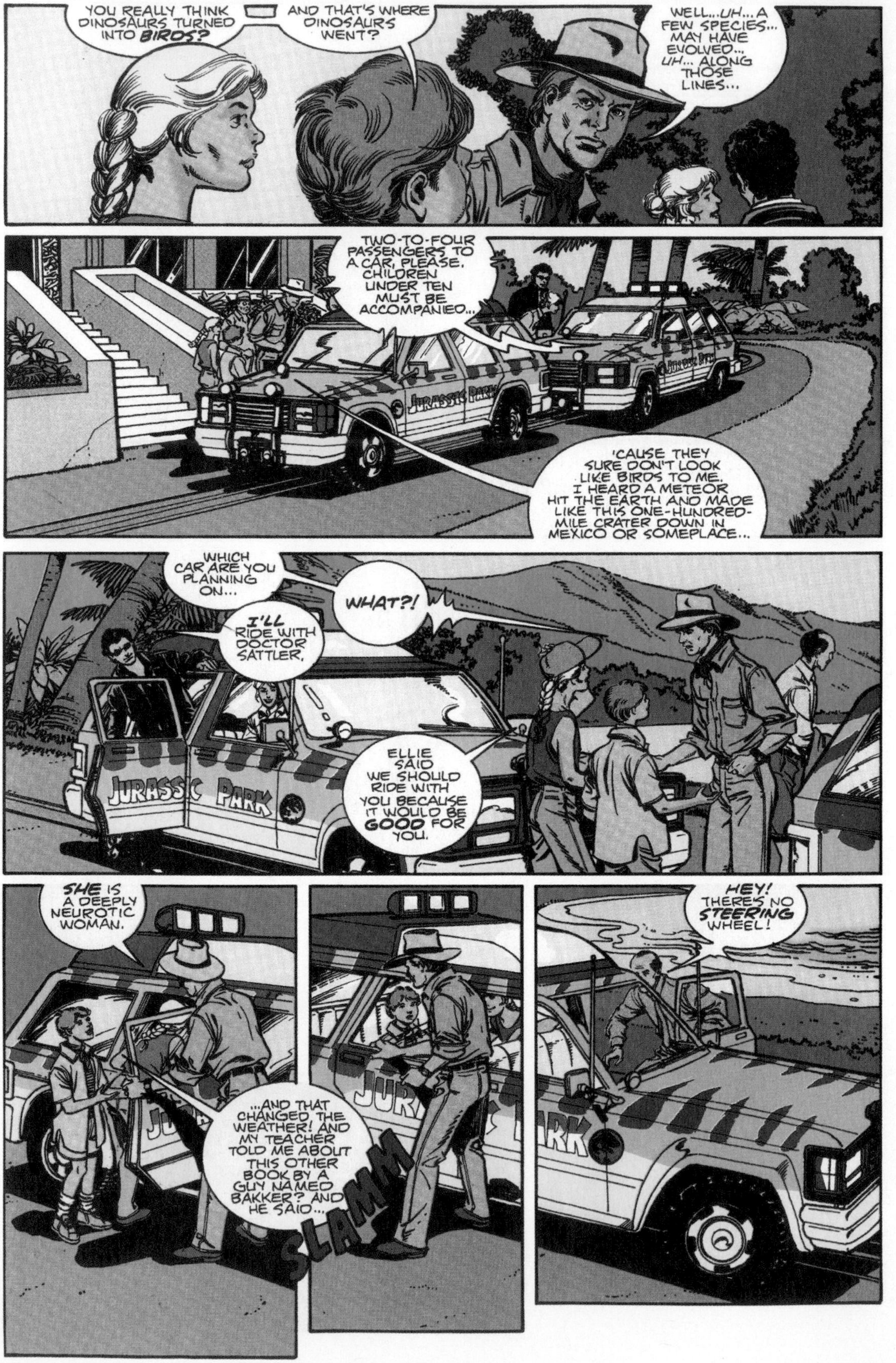
YOU REALLY THINK DINOSAURS TURNED INTO BIRDS?
AND THAT'S WHERE DINOSAURS WENT?
WELL... UH... A FEW SPECIES... MAY HAVE EVOLVED... UH... ALONG THOSE LINES...
TWO-TO-FOUR PASSENGERS TO A CAR, PLEASE. CHILDREN UNDER TEN MUST BE ACCOMPANIED...
JURASSIC PARK
'CAUSE THEY SURE DON'T LOOK LIKE BIRDS TO ME. I HEARD A METEOR HIT THE EARTH AND MADE LIKE THIS ONE-HUNDRED-MILE CRATER DOWN IN MEXICO OR SOMEPLACE...
WHICH CAR ARE YOU PLANNING ON...
WHAT?!
I'LL RIDE WITH DOCTOR SATTLER.
JURASSIC PARK
ELLIE SAID WE SHOULD RIDE WITH YOU BECAUSE IT WOULD BE GOOD FOR YOU.
SHE IS A DEEPLY NEUROTIC WOMAN.
...AND THAT CHANGED THE WEATHER! AND MY TEACHER TOLD ME ABOUT THIS OTHER BOOK BY A GUY NAMED BAKKER? AND HE SAID...
SLAMM
HEY! THERE'S NO STEERING WHEEL!

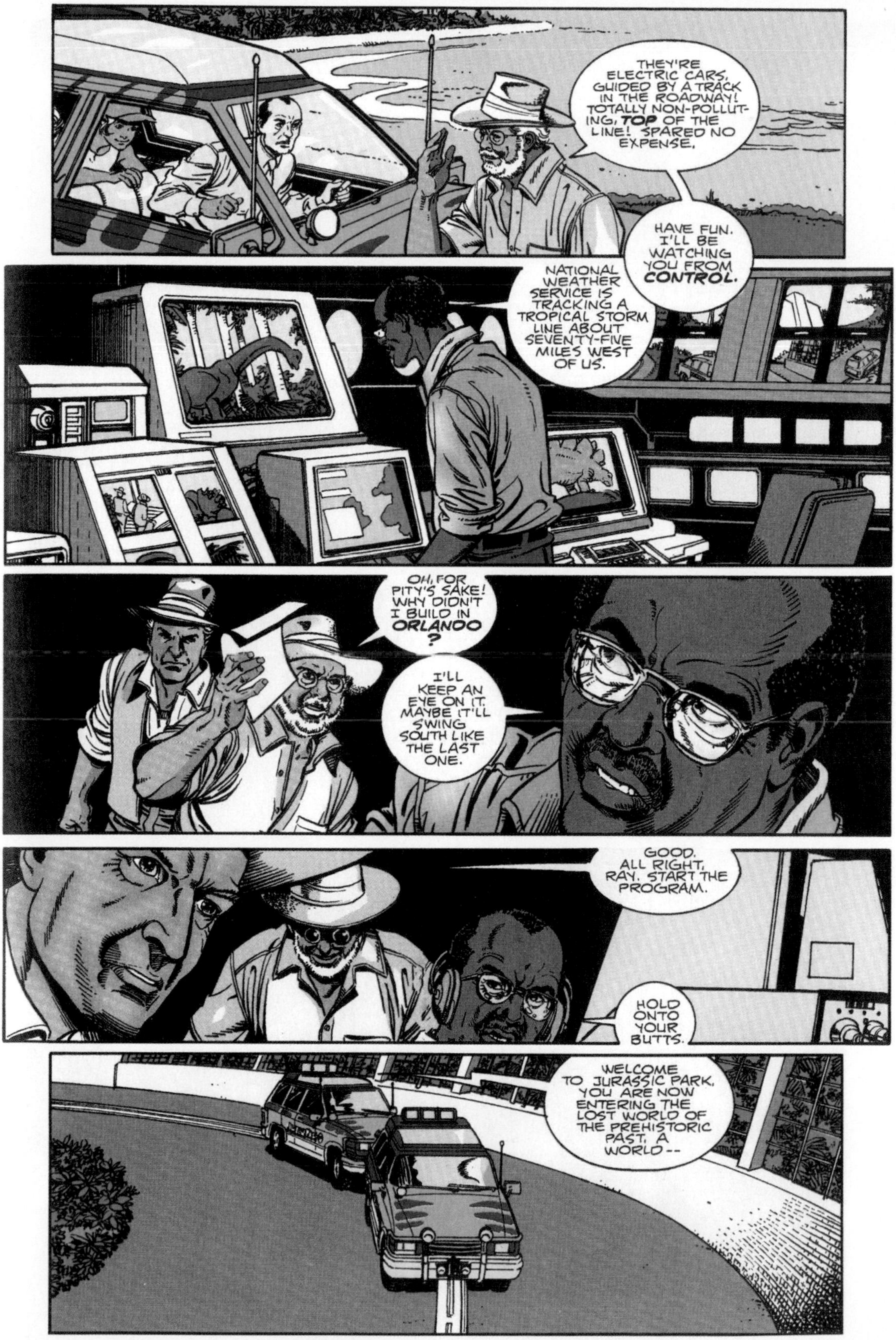
THEY'RE ELECTRIC CARS, GUIDED BY A TRACK IN THE ROADWAY! TOTALLY NON-POLLUTING, TOP OF THE LINE! SPARED NO EXPENSE.
HAVE FUN. I'LL BE WATCHING YOU FROM CONTROL.
NATIONAL WEATHER SERVICE IS TRACKING A TROPICAL STORM LINE ABOUT SEVENTY-FIVE MILES WEST OF US.
OH, FOR PITY'S SAKE! WHY DIDN'T I BUILD IN ORLANDO?
I'LL KEEP AN EYE ON IT. MAYBE IT'LL SWING SOUTH LIKE THE LAST ONE.
GOOD. ALL RIGHT, RAY. START THE PROGRAM.
HOLD ONTO YOUR BUTTS.
WELCOME TO JURASSIC PARK. YOU ARE NOW ENTERING THE LOST WORLD OF THE PREHISTORIC PAST. A WORLD--

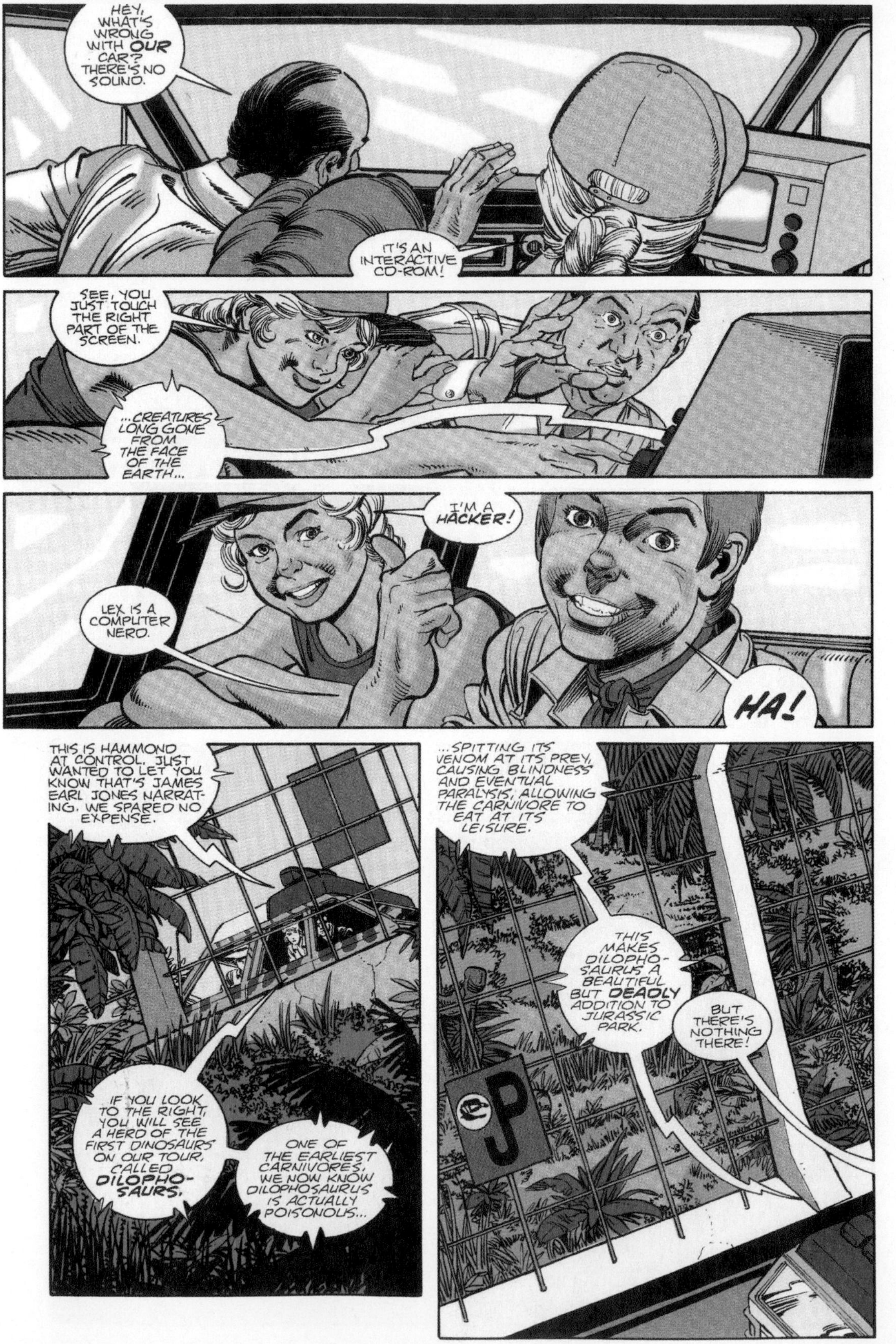
HEY, WHAT'S WRONG WITH **OUR** CAR? THERE'S NO SOUND.
IT'S AN INTERACTIVE CD-ROM!
SEE, YOU JUST TOUCH THE RIGHT PART OF THE SCREEN.
...CREATURES LONG GONE FROM THE FACE OF THE EARTH...
I'M A **HACKER!**
LEX IS A COMPUTER NERD.
HA!
THIS IS HAMMOND AT CONTROL. JUST WANTED TO LET YOU KNOW THAT'S JAMES EARL JONES NARRATING. WE SPARED NO EXPENSE.
IF YOU LOOK TO THE RIGHT, YOU WILL SEE A HERD OF THE FIRST DINOSAURS ON OUR TOUR, CALLED **DILOPHOSAURS.**
ONE OF THE EARLIEST CARNIVORES. WE NOW KNOW DILOPHOSAURUS IS ACTUALLY POISONOUS...
...SPITTING ITS VENOM AT ITS PREY, CAUSING BLINDNESS AND EVENTUAL PARALYSIS, ALLOWING THE CARNIVORE TO EAT AT ITS LEISURE.
THIS MAKES DILOPHOSAURUS A BEAUTIFUL BUT **DEADLY** ADDITION TO JURASSIC PARK.
BUT THERE'S NOTHING THERE!
JP

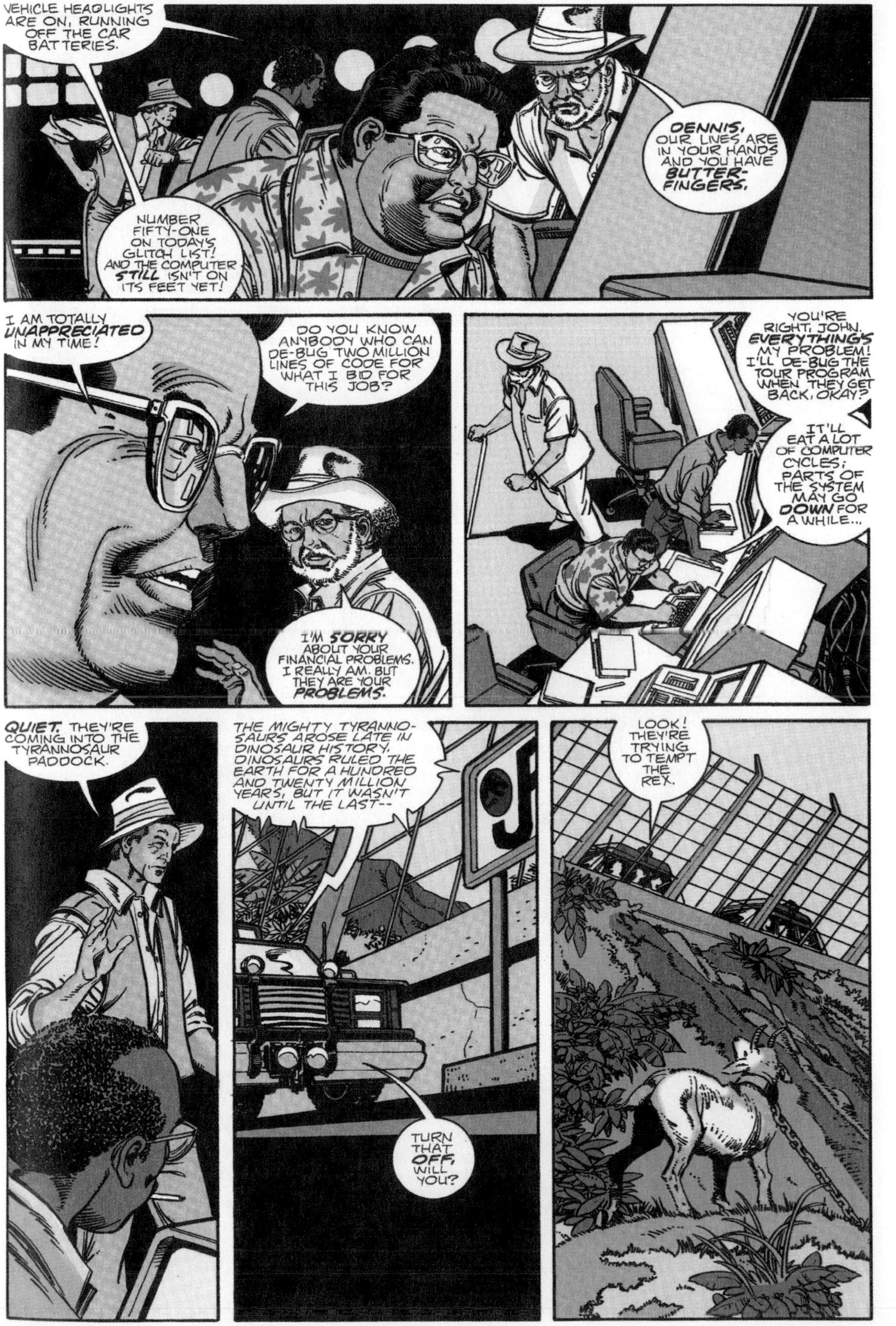
VEHICLE HEADLIGHTS ARE ON, RUNNING OFF THE CAR BATTERIES.
NUMBER FIFTY-ONE ON TODAY'S GLITCH LIST! AND THE COMPUTER STILL ISN'T ON ITS FEET YET!
DENNIS, OUR LIVES ARE IN YOUR HANDS AND YOU HAVE BUTTER-FINGERS.
I AM TOTALLY UNAPPRECIATED IN MY TIME!
DO YOU KNOW ANYBODY WHO CAN DE-BUG TWO MILLION LINES OF CODE FOR WHAT I BID FOR THIS JOB?
I'M SORRY ABOUT YOUR FINANCIAL PROBLEMS. I REALLY AM. BUT THEY ARE YOUR PROBLEMS.
YOU'RE RIGHT, JOHN. EVERYTHING'S MY PROBLEM! I'LL DE-BUG THE TOUR PROGRAM WHEN THEY GET BACK, OKAY?
IT'LL EAT A LOT OF COMPUTER CYCLES; PARTS OF THE SYSTEM MAY GO DOWN FOR A WHILE...
QUIET. THEY'RE COMING INTO THE TYRANNOSAUR PADDOCK.
THE MIGHTY TYRANNOSAURS AROSE LATE IN DINOSAUR HISTORY. DINOSAURS RULED THE EARTH FOR A HUNDRED AND TWENTY MILLION YEARS, BUT IT WASN'T UNTIL THE LAST--
TURN THAT OFF, WILL YOU?
LOOK! THEY'RE TRYING TO TEMPT THE REX.

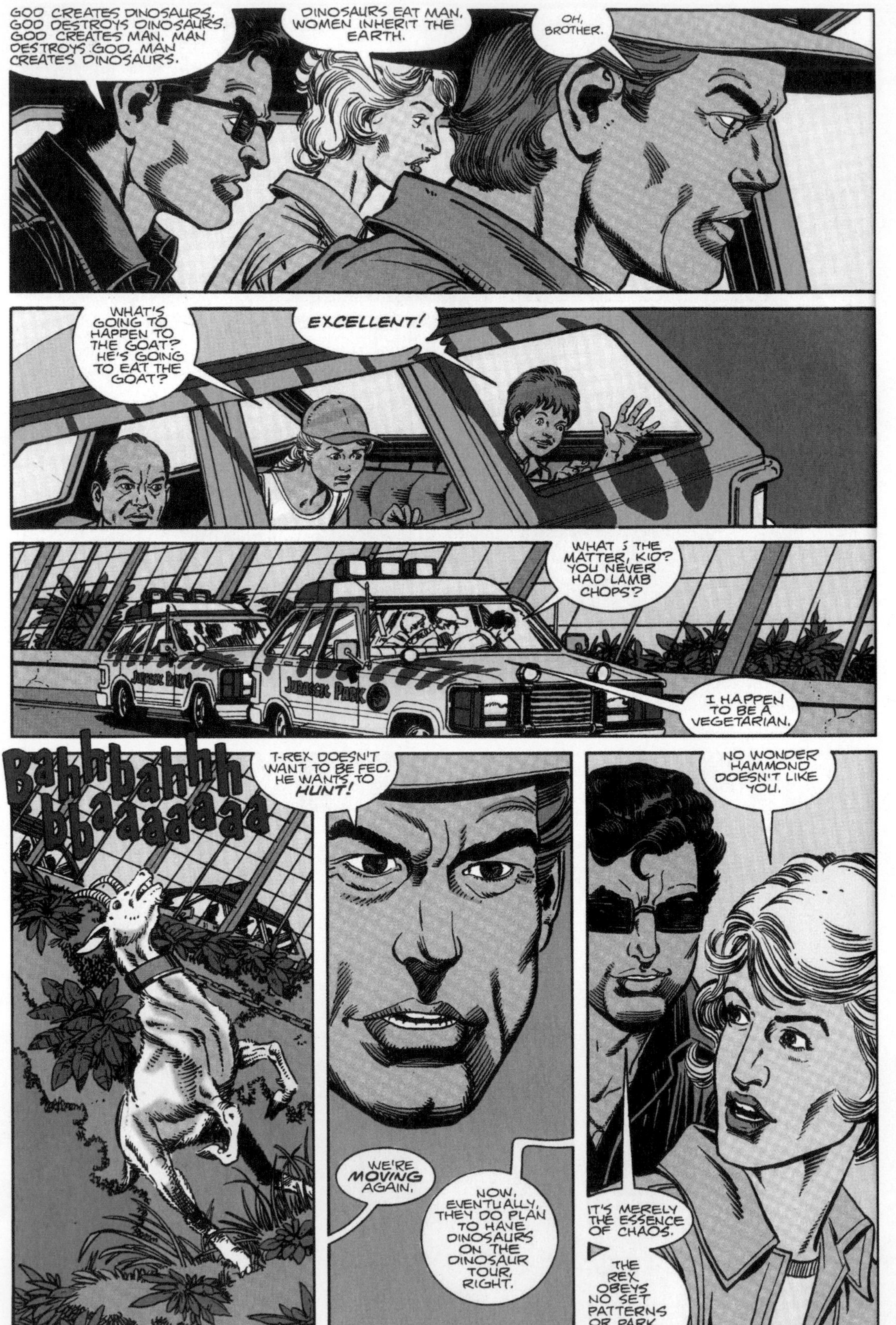
GOD CREATES DINOSAURS. GOD DESTROYS DINOSAURS. GOD CREATES MAN. MAN DESTROYS GOD. MAN CREATES DINOSAURS.
DINOSAURS EAT MAN. WOMEN INHERIT THE EARTH.
OH, BROTHER.
WHAT'S GOING TO HAPPEN TO THE GOAT? HE'S GOING TO EAT THE GOAT?
EXCELLENT!
WHAT'S THE MATTER, KID? YOU NEVER HAD LAMB CHOPS?
JURASSIC PARK
JURASSIC PARK
I HAPPEN TO BE A VEGETARIAN.
Bahhbahhh bbaaaaaaa
T-REX DOESN'T WANT TO BE FED. HE WANTS TO HUNT!
WE'RE MOVING AGAIN.
NOW, EVENTUALLY, THEY DO PLAN TO HAVE DINOSAURS ON THE DINOSAUR TOUR, RIGHT.
NO WONDER HAMMOND DOESN'T LIKE YOU.
IT'S MERELY THE ESSENCE OF CHAOS.
THE REX OBEYS NO SET PATTERNS OR PARK SCHEDULES.

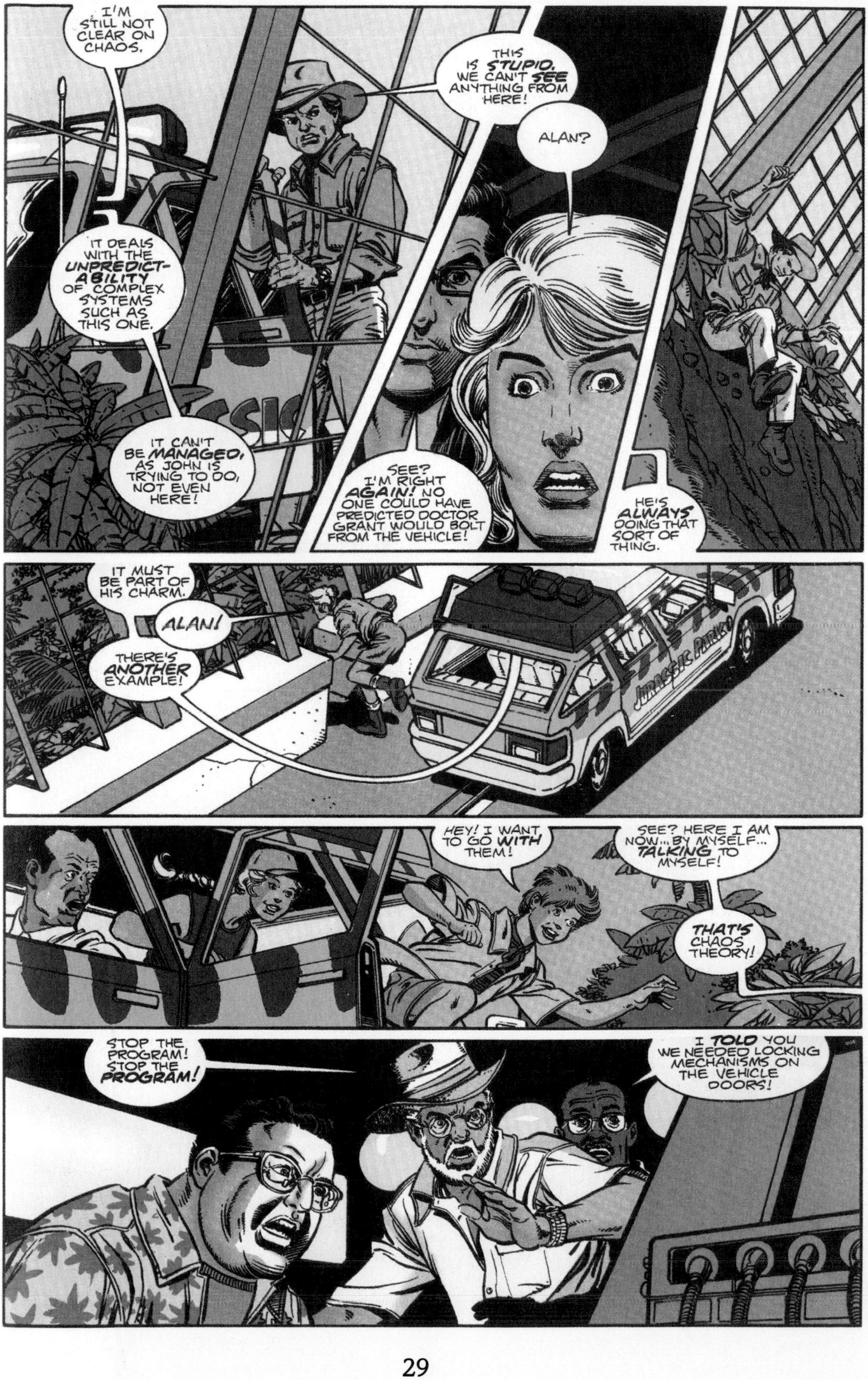
I'M STILL NOT CLEAR ON CHAOS.
THIS IS STUPID. WE CAN'T SEE ANYTHING FROM HERE!
ALAN?
IT DEALS WITH THE UNPREDICT-ABILITY OF COMPLEX SYSTEMS SUCH AS THIS ONE.
IT CAN'T BE MANAGED, AS JOHN IS TRYING TO DO, NOT EVEN HERE!
SEE? I'M RIGHT AGAIN! NO ONE COULD HAVE PREDICTED DOCTOR GRANT WOULD BOLT FROM THE VEHICLE!
HE'S ALWAYS DOING THAT SORT OF THING.
IT MUST BE PART OF HIS CHARM.
ALAN!
THERE'S ANOTHER EXAMPLE!
HEY! I WANT TO GO WITH THEM!
SEE? HERE I AM NOW... BY MYSELF... TALKING TO MYSELF!
THAT'S CHAOS THEORY!
STOP THE PROGRAM! STOP THE PROGRAM!
I TOLD YOU WE NEEDED LOCKING MECHANISMS ON THE VEHICLE DOORS!

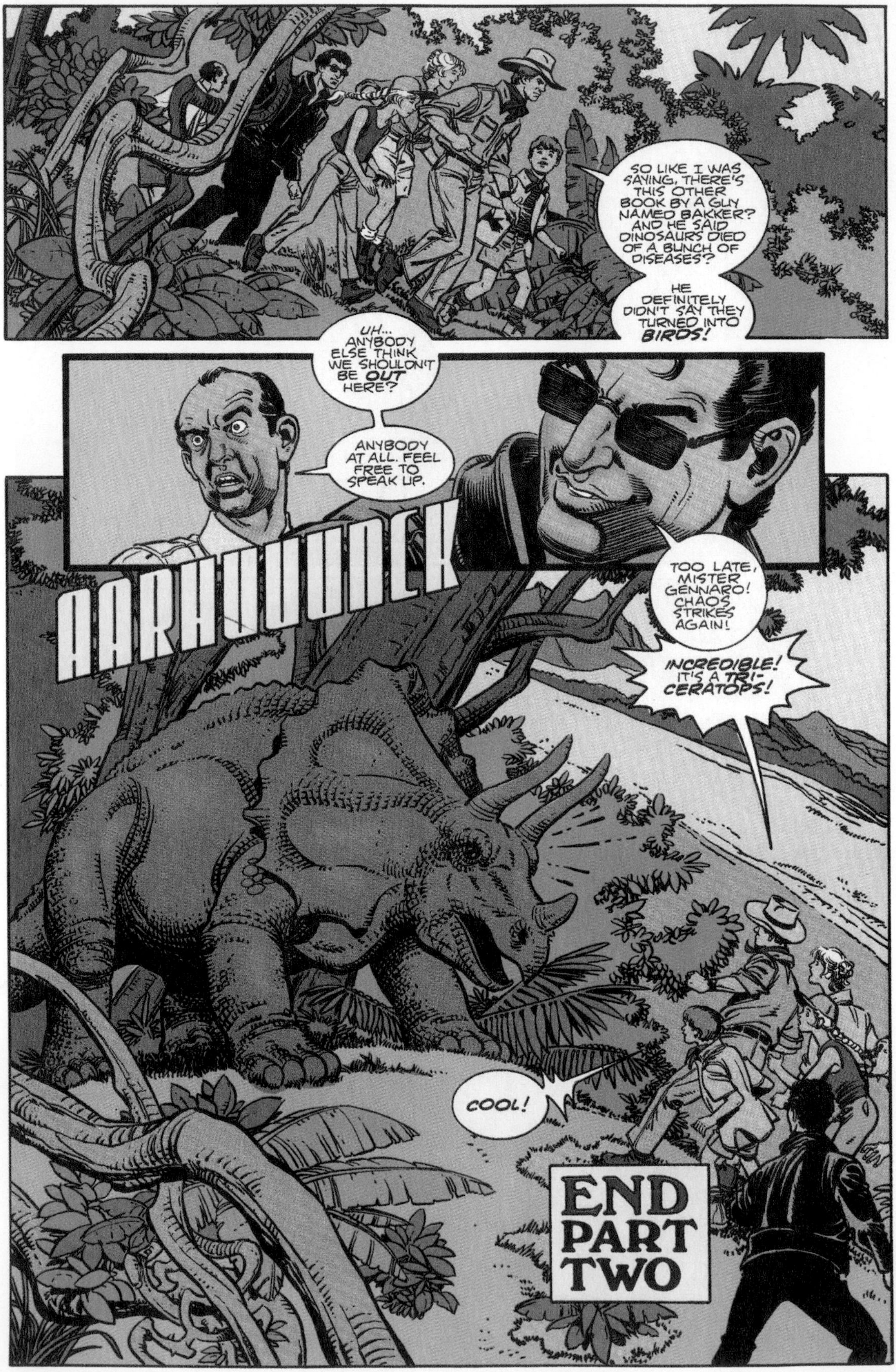
SO LIKE I WAS SAYING, THERE'S THIS OTHER BOOK BY A GUY NAMED BAKKER? AND HE SAID DINOSAURS DIED OF A BUNCH OF DISEASES?
HE DEFINITELY DIDN'T SAY THEY TURNED INTO BIRDS!
UH... ANYBODY ELSE THINK WE SHOULDN'T BE OUT HERE?
ANYBODY AT ALL. FEEL FREE TO SPEAK UP.
AARHUUUNCK
TOO LATE, MISTER GENNARO! CHAOS STRIKES AGAIN!
INCREDIBLE! IT'S A TRI-CERATOPS!
COOL!
END PART TWO